NDA

Introduction © 2022 Caitlin Forst
Text © 2022 the authors

Published in the United States by:
Archway Editions,
a division of powerHouse Cultural Entertainment, Inc.
32 Adams Street, Brooklyn, NY 11201

www.archwayeditions.us

Daniel Power, CEO
Chris Molnar, Editorial Director
Nicodemus Nicoludis, Managing Editor
Naomi Falk, Editor

Library of Congress Control Number: 2022940728

ISBN 978-1-57687-993-1

Printed by Toppan Leefung

First edition, 2022

10 9 8 7 6 5 4 3 2 1

Interior layout and design by Chris Molnar

Printed and bound in China

EDITIONS

NDA

AN AUTOFICTION ANTHOLOGY
EDITED BY CAITLIN FORST

Archway Editions, Brooklyn, NY

CONTENTS

EDITOR'S NOTE

Autofiction has recently been hit with moral, academic, and critical scrutiny.

I am not moral, academic, or a critic.

FIELD NOTES ON SUICIDE OR THE INABILITY TO COMMIT SUICIDE OR IT'S HARD TO FOLLOW A PO-MERANIAN AROUND

Vi Khi Nao

She has overstayed her welcome at Starbucks.

Starbucks closed at 10 p.m. At 10:05 p.m., she found herself approached by an impatient barista. The barista opened her mouth.

"We are closed."

"I know."

She finds her body parked outside Starbucks, at its incongruent parameter, near an un-threatening short cactus just shorter than her knees. She stood there gazing at the nocturnal, desolate traffic of the sinful but sinless city. Everything was sprawled out, including the air and its cars. People had already rushed home to eat their saturated-fat dinners with take-out burgers, fries, and decadent donuts, and to pre-pad their tummies with carbohydrate-dense pad thais. The lonesomeness of her existence makes the desolate landscape before her ache with desiccated, nocturnal residuum.

Time passes through her and around her.

At the parameter, she cries for three hours. When she cries, the wind is strong and her tears flutter away from her horizontally. The tears flutter like a scarf, ready to wrap themselves around the throat of Sin City, strangling it if they could. They are the kind of tears that are migratory and soundless. The city sleeps through her lachrymal profundity. The city won't let her commit suicide. She walks through a million different versions of how she could die or want to die.

Is it sinful to be trampled by a mini-van, by two adults on their way to the Bellagio to see the fountain dance the night away?

How does a person watch a city commit suicide and then get raped?

While climbing a small hill in New Mexico, another woman narrated to her a story about a dog who was kidnapped and raped in Mexico City. Her abductors wanted her to multiply their profits by forcing her to give birth, but her menstrual cycle hadn't arrived yet, at least not inside her body, and she was unable to reproduce. The abductors were in a hurry. The dog's owner had stapled reward pamphlets around the city and the abductors, how clever, returned the violated dog to the owner and she, in irony, gave the reward money to the abductors.

How does a city find itself amongst the different narrative structures of the city?

With which building should it ambush or clothe its soul?

When a city doesn't clothe itself in the nightmares of the past, what must a person who wishes to commit suicide but can't do?

A city sprawled out, waiting for a pamphlet to kiss it.

A city within a city, crawling around, wanting a good fuck.

Who is willing to fuck it?

Will it have any good luck?

Sin City will tell you all about it. About its time sleeping with Donald Trump, Steve Wynn, Andre Agassi, Jenna Jameson, Chelsie Hightower, and Stevenson Sylvester.

A tennis ball rolls down a hill. Its path is dictated by gravity, not volition. The violation is in its silence, once the ball loses its kinetic momentum when the city doesn't turn its hips or shoulders or its arms so the ball could accelerate more. Its volition is in its silence, not its resilience. Who is capable of destroying whom?

"I was a camel owner before I was a dog owner," says the desert as it watches the child of Mexico City rape a dog. The desert is not a rolling tongue. In the heat, wetness is a luxury, which the tongue can afford but not the landscape. There are myriad ways to intellectualize, to culturalize, to educate momentum and human velocity (not ball velocity). The ferociousness of a blind tennis ball.

The human spirit rolls down a city, with or without gravity or momentum. Its enemy isn't the tennis ball. Its enemy is itself. Its enemy is the climate of change, which climbs the backs of all mountain lions. At night, the wind howls and cries and even the human spirit gets weathered and weakened by the sound of the city dumbed-down by sinless gambling and tactless cocktails. She cries in front of the city, her back to Starbucks.

Is it luck or is it noise that she considers suicide? It is not her last resort. Her last resort is to return home. To climb into bed. To enter an empty apartment without fish sauce inside.

An inferior soul is a soul that decides to change its shirt from blue to white after a change of climate.

An inferior soul is an Impala after it pulls out of the driveway of a house that has spent a night sleeping in the cremation of a dream.

An inferior soul is a bottle of water that has withdrawn its membership from a watermelon orchard.

A superior soul knows when it is winter and when it will snow.

Outside, the mud remembers a young dog, a pomeranian, who ran away from Iran because somewhere in its heritage is the Caspian Sea and the Persian gulf, with an approximately population of 66 millions, not dog population.

Before 1979, Iran was a monarchy.

Before 1979, the young pomeranian was the progeny of a rapist.

Before 1979, was there an Iranian in a pomeranian?

So began the Iran-Iraq War.

And then in 2001, the US got involved in a very romantic relationship with a fake nuclear psychoanalyst called Afghanistan.

A superior soul knows when to adopt an Iranian pomearanian and how to not start a deja-vu-esque, quasi, post-repetitive Vietnam War with the Middle East.

Outside, a water pump is in the midst of being built, and maybe a gas station that sells Doritos.

Meanwhile, a rose bush is manually lit on fire.

And Moses tells Aaron that he is hired to be his own White House correspondent and the Sea God asks him to part its non-nuclear weapon, i.e. technology. Facebook, mainly.

EXCERPT from AND IF I COULD, I TRULY WOULD

Rindon Johnson

I wear the leather sometimes before I leave it outside. I climb into it and wrap it around me, I pull it open and try to lie on its creases to make it flat and then I lie next to it. I draw on it. I try and photograph it. I cover it in Vaseline to try and keep it moist. I hold it in my hand and I think about its head holes. Diamond mentioned that a woman told her that birthmarks are wounds from your previous life. Sometimes the cows and I have similar birthmarks, A white cow had a small kite like I do on the back of my neck. A brown cow for a sofa doesn't have any birthmarks because in the process of becoming leather for a sofa most birthmarks are dyed and evened out. I look much better in the summer because I'm darker and you cannot see all my scars. I apply a lot of I statements to the leather in person. Other times, I don't do anything in my own person, I write emails and have phone calls and ask people I know to buy leather and put it outside. Then I talk to the person about the leather all the time and they tell me about it and I wrap it around me from afar.

In the car again, this time you are driving, the sun is exactly over my head and we have just come over a ridge on the tarred markless road. I say: they're called Joshua Trees because mormons saw them and immediately knew they were praying like Joshua. What does praying look like if you are not Joshua and you were not there to see him praying?

You laugh: Clearly, it means to pray extravagantly upward. Obviously.

The story of Joshua is as follows:

Moses dies before the Israelites can reach the promised land. Joshua takes over as leader of the Israelites. If you remember, there were already people living on the promised land then too. They were called the Cannites but they lived in sin so they deserved no land. The Israelites fought many battles for the promised land, the battles that they won were battles that God won for them, they surrendered to God and he delivered them victories. For the final battle, Joshua sends spies into the Promised Land and they convert some Cannites. The spies, the converted and the Israelites take over the city from within the city like a parasite or virus. All one, the Israelites finally crossed the river, Jordan, like they crossed the red sea, it parted. When they arrive, Joshua has an encounter with a strange warrior, who unbeknownst to Joshua turns out to be the Angel Commander of God's army. Joshua asks the Commander Angel, are you with us or are you against us. The angel says, Neither. Was Joshua praying to understand the place of his people within a binary of his own making? Do we pray to Joshua to learn how to surrender?

On my way to you on a full enough moon, I am surrounded by Windmills, the giant 21st century kind, whose blades often cut birds in half mid flight. The makers are trying to mitigate this, their success rates vary. There are a lot of dead birds. Jordan says a dead bird in your path means a death is coming. The windmills have red lights on them and in the darkness I can only make out the outline of the blades as the lights are blinking intermittently in their rows, like one row seems to blink or every few seems to blink, it goes blades, red light, darkness. Climbing higher into the mountains towards you, I took this long turn this heavy long turn, slowly driving upward at an angle, red lights getting larger, surrounding me as though I was becoming them or something like this.

I give the leather titles which are actually something else. For now I consider them the other line that marks the area of the work, a limit of a sphere or activity. Between is my hand, the butcher, the cow, the vat, the skin, the vinegar, the dirt, and so on. I'm getting ahead of myself. For example, here is a title:

Little Prometheus: Roughly I have been following the coordinate curves but where did they come thru the ceiling round, in day time a particular shade of yellow (white) at dusk the orange of Success Academy uniforms, my mom says those kids look like who done it, well what for, roughly fore now, too bad about money, what about something else living, I will, I do, the largest moth in the world, lye in bed with you, green everything, take your shoes off, typhoon, make silk storm shelters, harden, look to the horizon, hatch when it passes, fly miles for the smell of them, don't have mouths, never eat

rust, rawhide

Driving upstate to go to graduate school, an accident occurs in front of me. A gold sedan spins out of control, flying forward across the two lanes, it flips, still spinning, hard on its top, the car teeters back and forth before settling, crushing the metal further. Somehow in the time that it took for the car to loose control and flip, the human being driving the car disappeared within the car so by the time that my fellow drivers and I regained consciousness from the hypnosis of the flipping it felt as though there was no longer a human within the car, just a car. Frozen, parked on the free way, we look around at one another. Two motorcyclists in front of me jump off their bikes, one directs traffic, the other cautiously inspects the car. Gently, but gruffly, the motorcyclist directing traffic tells me to call 911. I do, I don't know where I am, the woman on the phone finds where I am located, she thanks me and tells me to have a wonderful day. I drive around the accident and I think about the clear difference in time between when there was a person in the car and when there was no longer a person in the car - did the person become the car? Where have they gone?

Later recounting all of this, other People keep saying to me, that when someone dies, after they weigh nothing.

Oh them, is this now?

Stand by yourself then
good looking
deformed
lengthy
voluminous.

I read the catalog essay for an exhibition of Ana Mendieta's work. I mourn her all the time when I am making things. What would she have become I wonder? The essay reads: She was surely convinced, that language and knowledge were at the same time, liberty and oppression, in so much as they constitute the most precious weapons for both the oppressor and the oppressed.[1]

Driving from my native San Francisco to Los Angeles down interstate 5 the landscape is usually yellow and dry, but somehow (rain) when I'm driving to see you, the 5 is verdant, it looks like somewhere not California. I have been driving or been driven on the 5 for my entire life and the cows remain. I can smell them before I see them. What does it mean to leave someone outside? What do I expect of them? I'm trying to translate all of this. This is a pain. Was your winter cold? Mine was very hot. Do we save the planet. I don't like the word radical, I do not think I have within me a great refusal (Marcuse). I can smell them before I see them. Feeding in the left of my eye (giving little to the window) and then fully formed in my rear view mirror, feasting on corn bread and cardboard, standing in their own sour, black shit, tails swinging away the flys. A friend describes another friend in a spiral. His skin started to look bad, and he is always wasted, now that I think about it he smells bad. I keep driving. I am hungry. I go to in-n-out. Sir. Mr. Johnson. What would you like.² I eat a cheeseburger, sloppy, alone in the car.

Sappho via Carson,
I don't know what to do
Two states of mind me.[3]

You say when I come home and my front door is ajar:
Even particular people leave doors open.

Pardon our work. There was immense fear that we would become part of a senseless butchery.

For example (title): They are running together because they sink up together, it feels like they are running slower but they are actually running faster, they are running faster together

Vaseline, Ebonizing (Coffee) Dye, Furniture Leather

My partner and I watch Coming to America and she declares it the perfect movie. It is the perfect movie, mostly because it is completely of it's time, further, it is not so much Coming to America as Coming from Black America. The pan-African 80's royalness which Eddie Murphy wears nonchalantly, as though he really was born Prince Akim of Zamunda manifests in his quoting of Nietzsche, a natural hair rat tail, hair sustained by juices and berries and flower bearers to drop flower petals where ever he walks. It is a fairy tale. Under the guise of sowing his royal Oats, Prince Akim goes to Queens to find his queen. There he discovers being poor and black in New York in 1988. Somehow, the poverty, burning buildings and his minimum wage job look just fine through the eyes of the ever smiling young Prince who, when all of this is over, can go back to his palace in Africa.

We are driving to go see Black Panther and after we see the movie I am freaked out. Are you ok, you ask me. Obviously.

What propositions can I offer that have no basis in any known form or language?

Surrender:

I am thinking about Coming to America when we leave Black Panther. What Afro-futurist dream space is Black Panther in comparison to the flat, easy, wouldn't it be nice world of Coming to America. In Black Panther, the sumptuous landscapes, rituals and costumes of fictional black royalty somehow stumble into a confusing-anti-communist-anti-black-american-precious-metal-trade-war-spiral. Again, American blackness is a commodity served to me and at times I thoroughly enjoy it, at others I am a goose whose liver will become foie gras, never hungry, mouth open to the sky, eyes bulging. What I am saying is that the craziest part about this economic system is that a film designed to win the support of those who have been oppressed by the economic system depicts and promotes more of their oppression by the economic system. We byproducts are products, are consumers and the whole time we are actually someone else.

Now that I am called Sir, I realize that I am beginning to publicly exist all the way in the between - they all know now. (Possible Memoir Book Titles: AS IF SEEING IS KNOWING or A BOY WITH A WOMAN'S HANDS A SMALL VOICE.)

We leave the theater and I stare up at the Joshua Tree in someone else's yard - we don't get too close because it is dangerous to look like us in other people's yards. I ask looking up at the Joshua tree, are you for us or against us. Obviously, the tree answers, neither.

Neither, nor. What then?

Why does it seem like when cows die they are still heavy?

My hands have been very Ashy lately, insatiable and thirsty. I have not tried very hard to quench their thirst as I am generally negligent with my body and other bodies. I use leather and it smells good at first but then it begins to smell terrible. A skin without a body is called a hide. We both scar and can be branded. I am very interested in skin, in it's weathering and color. A friend, the other day said that I was working with organs. Organs are porous and permeable. How deep, what happens.

I have to get to the other side of the animal.[4]

Driving, thinking of the cows, I am thinking about methane gas. Methane is leaking from the permafrost. My partner is from Australia and she says meth-ane, ME-thane. They are thinking about cloning wooly mammoths to pound down the permafrost, naturally, this is ethically confusing. Obviously one thing leads to another thing. My dad says that ethics are useless to markets. You cannot approach a market with ethics. A market is not a being. If the body is used to entertain is the body then part of the market and so then the market becomes a being? (A Large One.) My dad used this example: what is the point of worrying about getting wet if you've already been swimming and there is no sun. Well you're already wet and you're not going to dry.

Me. Me. Me. Me. Me. Me. Me.

Recently with my sculptures I have been making dyes to make them brown, black, blue, like me. These dyes also make them generally light sensitive, sometimes I add photo emulsion. I leave the sculptures outside. I am taking photographs of dirt, with dirt and time. Time is also a form of dirt or sand or particles. Moving around in all the dirt and time I worried for a moment I was a land artist and in that time period I read a little bit of Smithson, I read a little bit of Lucy Lippard and then I kept reading her. Mostly I read about these artists rituals overlaid upon prehistoric rituals. In Overlay, she doesn't mean to but somehow the rituals of the artists feel so small and drastic in comparison to their ancient referents. There is a lot too about gender. Lucy was thinking about gender. I suppose I am too. Men seem to crawl into holes in the dirt and every now and then, despite the "void" in her jeans, a woman makes something incredible. Gender feels so relevant to Lucy and so relevant to me too. Relevant in that I don't understand it and I generally despise it, but I participate. I participate in consumption too. Sometimes I eat meat. I think about the methane and the mammoths and then I eat the meat because I'm hungry and iron deficient and I don't have time to think about much of anything other than my deficiencies. They're loud.[5]

I am a byproduct of the market so then I too am the market?

Ok Objectivity, let's see who you really are… Subjectivity! It was you all along.

Is then what this is from?

What happens when my feast is dependent on another's undoing (reworking)?

Have you ever tried to photograph the moon?

At Home Depot I passed him in the aisle and as I passed him, I saw that his arm and shoulder had been badly burned, the skin, in its healing had turned pink, yellow, waxy, heavy and rendering his arm small in comparison to his large, strong body. I desired his arm so much in that moment I was rendered speechless, he became simply his arm and my eyes feasted. Then I bought a rubber mallet, went back to the studio and finished my installation.

We've been here before.
We haven't.
We have.
That was somebody else.
It was you.
It wasn't.
We continue.
We haven't been here before together.
We have.
That was somebody else.
It was you.
It was not.
Drop it I say.
You don't.
Then I don't.
We've never been here before together.

We have.
We have not.
You don't remember this?
We've never been here before together.

Since we disagree nothing is quite true. I realize smoking weed later that this is maybe what it is like to be alive or to remember. Nothing is quite anything if your stories don't match. Did that really happen, I have the scar, I found a receipt in my pocket, my clothes smell like the woods.

Is then what this is from?

For example (title): You don't want the light you want the moon, the moon will reflect the scales, you take your gig, which is like a spear and flounders are so flat that you just see their reflection and then you take your spear and seek the reflection and then you have a flounder.

Vaseline, Ebonizing (Coffee) Dye, Photo Emulsion, Leather

Works Cited

Kuspit, Donald B., and Gloria Moure. Ana Mendieta. Ediciones Polígrafa, 1996.

Lippard, Lucy R. Overlay: Contemporary Art and the Art of Prehistory. The New Press, 2010.

Reines, Ariana. The Cow. Fence Books, 2017.

Sappho, and Anne Carson. If Not, Winter: Fragments of Sappho. Vintage Books, 2003.

Notes

1. Kuspit, Donald B., and Gloria Moure. Ana Mendieta. Ediciones Polígrafa, 1996.

2. Conversation, Passing @ In-n-Out Burger, Los Banos California, March 8th, 2018

3. Sappho, and Anne Carson. If Not, Winter: Fragments of Sappho. Vintage Books, 2003.

4. Reines, Ariana. The Cow. Fence Books, 2017.

5. Lippard, Lucy R. Overlay: Contemporary Art and the Art of Prehistory. The New Press, 2010.

DOG WASHED BLUE

Nathan Dragon

Internal Clock

Practice staying half-busy keeping track of the ways daylight savings can and cannot affect a dog.

And maybe I'll come to some understanding.

Like when it gets dark the dog sits—I know what he wants. He wants dinner, because to him, it gets dark the same time every day.

Woodpecker

I still haven't seen a woodpecker here—but I'm holding out.

This has been my least favorite place to live the last 5 years. I've seen woodpeckers everywhere else. Flickers in Massachusetts and Chicago, that big pileated woodpecker in Western Mass., and the Gila in Tucson.

I think I know the kinds that live here, some are the same as anywhere. I think I know what to look for.

Stick a Finger Into It

In a dish of vinegar in the kitchen, fruit flies bob around a blue drop of Dawn.

A question I've never had the answer to: where do they come from?

Still learning that less is more and sometimes none is best.

Stick a finger into the soil, up to around the first knuckle, water a plant if it needs it. We have 3 plants "for air quality".

I want to be outside more. But not sure how to do it.

I used to want to be a marine biologist because I imagined you just get paid to go swimming or snorkeling—which, you know, is still swimming in plenty of ways.

A friend told me that for whenever you want to swim but can't get to a pool or lake, you should take a long shower.

Moving

A thought that occurs to me at least once on long drives, briefly, or if things are going bad, or if I'm bored, or if the landscape is boring or sad: Why are long drives romanticized?

Pool

I remember the feeling of hitting my head at the bottom of the pool.

Midwestern City

Once I watched glass shatter off the side of a special glass-transportation van right before the interstate overpass at California Avenue.

Light green-blue like a flat wave breaking all over the gray pavement. It was the color of schooling chromis or water boiling around a coral reef.

Gum Wrappers

One possible combination: a lot of romanticism, no idealism, and little to no irony either. Something about meeting expectations realistically and *if appearance is everything*—what are the odds?—if you look at it this way—of, I don't know, breaking the safe.

Growing up I knew this kid who rolled joints using gum wrappers that he scraped bright blue foil off of.

Pumpkin

There's a 99cent pumpkin in the window. Still holding up. Fresh, solid, orange.

The other night my mouth felt sticky from a hip and bitter drink, and thinking about it now makes my teeth feel weird. This was somebody's new take where the only thing the same was the orange peel. I tried not to say anything when it was offered. I took it and I drank it.

Here

I remember another thing from being a kid: peeing the toilet foamy. I gotta remember to try next time I pee.

But I can't control what I think when I pee. I automatically end up perusing rummage sale memories of sentimental objects—the sea-green glider, the white and dough peel, the things' memories of meals made, bottoms held, palimpsesting evidence of a past life or past lives. All the things that have been given away, to the church-charity thrift stores, or as hand-me-downs, things sold at yard sales or flea markets, traded at swap meets.

I think, Why did I get rid of everything I wished I'd kept. And why'd I keep a bunch of junk I don't know why I've kept?

And sometimes I end up talking to myself saying something I just made up, but also something I really could have said at some point in time: "How was the weather there Friday? I've been wanting to head up there to drop a few things off and take a swim in the lake."

Gone Fishin'

There are a handful of signs I wish to experience unironically.

A sign in the window of the market in town.

Then, one day, a comeback tour.

An oscillative statement: "It is what it is."

Picking up all the hairs I've pulled out. It's embarrassing.

Pathetic Fallacy

The wind missed the chimes completely so they sit silently. There's a sundial in a box somewhere in one of the stacks of boxes around. The dog, wetted blue, stopped barking then started up again. Been like this the last 3 nights. Meanwhile I had some applesauce and a dandelion tea.

Errand Weather

One day this week I needed it to be nice out for an errand. I'd been crossing my fingers for a little green and yellow weather, muted and slightly subdued if possible. Good light to put things away in for a little while.

Made a list, slid on some boots.

Knew I forgot to shut something off.

"What can you really say? — No, to that!"

The dark brown wood of an old episode of People's Court.

Dog-sleep slowness.

Seltzer water and tropically flavored antacids.

Honeycured and heading into something.

Productive Day In

Opened the windows.

The smell of hairspray is coming through the vents. I just vacuumed all the dusty corners. Window sills.

Sitting down for a sec, thinking—Why the fuck do I do that.

From this angle, the tree looks like it will snap in the wind. I'm uncomfortable about yesterday.

And deciding how much to take and where to put the rest and why to put the rest. Thinking about a pile of things called: Why Do I Even Have This? Or Why Do I Still Have This? — Not to be confused with I Didn't Know I Still Had This. One organizational decision after another.

Symmetry

When I boxed it was 1) boxer 2) trainer 3) conerman 4) cut man.

And at the pizza shop it was 1) pizza 2) grill 3) counter 4) prep.

Blue

In the blue room I call the office I'm reminded of a thought I have frequently: Why can't these new energy saving light bulbs look the same as the old energy wasting light bulbs? Like if technology is so advanced.

I've stopped using this room.

The light in the other rooms and the smell and the stillness of the air fits better for the time being. Warm air in the light that slotted downwards to a warm spot on the floor where the blue dog is lying down and drying off.

Calculated Risk/Reward

Every time I light the candle I think about how the bottle of hand sanitizer next to it might blow.

THE TROUBLES

Brad Phillips

In 1984 a bad thing happened to my high-school girlfriend. Twenty-five years later I pulled off a karmic intervention that, while not undoing what happened to Hannah (who in 1984 was not my high school girlfriend but instead a nine-year-old living in her parents' van in an empty lot near Naropa University in Boulder, Colorado), may have, had she not taken her own life in 1995, provided her with some sense of comfort, or if not comfort, the comfort of revenge. Exacting revenge is almost always a comforting feeling. Or, having committed many acts of revenge, I, Brad Phillips find it comforting, while others might find it painful, unfulfilling, unsatisfactory, or, something they wish they could take back, as acts of revenge sometimes result in punitive actions being taken against the revenge seeker, contingent on the style of revenge they take.

(grammar-monster.com states that, "to **avenge** means to take **vengeance** on behalf of another. To **revenge** means to take satisfaction by carrying out a retributive action.")

I met and lost my virginity to Hannah in 1991. I was seventeen, she was sixteen. I later discovered that Hannah herself was not a virgin, at least not physiognomically, due to the perverse and abusive actions of a bad uncle. A bad uncle is someone who has existed and caused heartache in the family of almost every single woman I've ever known. In a world free of consequence, while it may sound extreme and many innocents would die, I would support a legion of extremely moral people, accompanied by psychopaths and mercenaries, undertaking an ethnic cleansing of sorts, where the ethnicity is simply 'uncle.'

My veins course with the blood of the Northern Irish. Many of my great uncles and second and third cousins were members of the Irish Republican Army. When people call me British or English, I get upset. I was taught to hate the English from birth. It's possible my grandfather, while my mother changed my diaper, held photographs of Queen Elizabeth in my face and tore them in half. My grandmother often referred to Prince Philip as a 'faggot' and 'diddler'. Elizabeth was simply, 'that fucking cunt'. In Canada Elizabeth's face defaces every coin, including those in my pocket right now. As a child, whenever I lost a tooth I'd find a coin from the Tooth Fairy under my pillow with Queen Elizabeth's face obscured by a piece of black electrical tape.

I once lived in Vancouver. My best friend and I, along with his girlfriend Rose, were walking to an art opening. A group of drunk jocks approached us. An atmosphere of hostility erupted immediately, and as the jocks passed us, one spit in Rose's face. We instinctively took a moment to comfort her before running to attack the jock who'd spat on her. Sadly we were too late, he'd already gotten into a car and was pulling away. I had a bicycle which I mounted, managing to keep up with the car as I followed it through Chinatown until it parked. I sat on my bicycle under a tree in the dark, trying to assess the best way to deal with the situation. The jocks exited the car and were greeted by a larger group of jocks exiting the house they'd parked in front of. The jocks all fist bumped and chest bumped and crushed beer cans then went back into the home. There were too many jocks for me alone to contend with. I went back to get my best friend, who shared the name Jack with John F. Kennedy, the Irish president of the United States whose head was blown off by Woody Harrelson's father (hidden behind a manhole type grate beneath the street where the road meets the curb) at the behest of Lyndon Johnson, who once had his own sister killed. We returned to jock headquarters and hid across the street in a shadowed gap between streetlamps with our bicycles. The jocks remained inside, listening to Nickleback and assumedly sexually assaulting women. I tapped Jack on the back and said,

"I've got an idea."

I did have an idea. I slipped off my shoes and took off my socks, then tied them together turning the pair into one long piece of absorptive fabric. Then I put my shoes back on. While Jack kept watch I walked across the street and opened the gas cap of the car the spitter had driven. I pushed my doubled sock into the gas tank and within thirty seconds the entire thing was soaked in gasoline. Next I pulled half the sock out of the gas tank, took out my lighter, lit the end on fire and ran back to Jack. Being soaked in gasoline the sock took to the fire like a fly to a corpse. We both lit cigarettes and before exhaling the first drag the car, an Acura Integra, exploded. The explosion was enormous, far bigger than I'd expected and therefore more satisfying. The sound of frightened jocks filled the night air. As they poured out of the house I saw the spitter was in tears. They looked at each other with confusion, maybe hoping that as friends they might comfort one another - an impossibility due to their intense homophobia. They all seemed desperate for a hug, shattered by the abuse the Acura had suffered. Jack and I felt very good, very satisfied. In the overwhelming frenzy of repressed jock emotion and roaring fire we quietly drove our bicycles back to Jack's house, where we smoked marijuana and watched *Law & Order*. We'd avenged Rose, but even more so, we'd exacted vengeance on the type of male (useless, unnecessary in this world, causing only pain and suffering, throwing our planet further into the abyss by continuing to reproduce) that had tormented us when we were children and teenagers. This particular act, the use of a piece of fabric to absorb gasoline and blow up a car is called,

"An Irish Parking Ticket".

The first time we had sex Hannah began screaming two minutes into what would've been a two minute and thirty second act. I'd of course heard how it was painful for a woman to lose her virginity, that the hymen was a thick wall of tissue I had no choice but to obliterate, something I felt guilty about in advance. But when Hannah screamed, the perforation of her tissue by my fledgling dick was not the first thing that crossed my mind. I instead assumed I sucked so much at fucking that in her disappointment, Hannah bypassed yawning, sighing and laughing and went directly to screaming. This illustrates the depths of insecurity I felt about my sex style and set the tone for subsequent encounters with girls. The next year I was told that in fact I did know how to fuck, and this came from Sandy Kowalchuk, the self-proclaimed slut of Dunbarton High School and therefore a certifiable validator of male sexual expertise. I'd known girls to be called sluts before (often by other girls), Sandy was the first I'd ever heard designate herself as such. Slut at that age simply meant that she'd fucked at least once. Sandy'd also allegedly given Mike Piche a blowjob during lunch in the back of his pickup in the Burger King parking lot. Or this is what she said. Sandy's assertion of her own sluttiness in hindsight reminds me of the story many young boys have told, for perhaps hundreds of years and across the globe. They claim to have a very hot girlfriend in a neighbouring town who they fingerbanged over summer break, and with whom they were having a very lurid epistolary relationship, just waiting until that moment when they could be reunited. Alan Blakely for example had such a girlfriend in New Hampshire who he'd met at a Math Olympics in Concord over spring break. He later changed schools when it was discovered that his big-titted trigonometric sex machine was in fact a model whose photograph adorned the packaging of duotangs widely available in Grand & Toy shops throughout the northeast. Alan's father cut his lawn with a pair of scissors. During my first year of college Alan was arrested for sexually molesting young boys in a wading pool where he worked as a lifeguard. We all should have known; the warning signs were there. In grade ten he'd broken into the McDonald's he was assistant manager of (at two in the morning) to make Whoppers for his tight circle of ten-year-old friends. Alan was fifteen and had put on his McDonald's uniform before breaking into the restaurant.

Sandy wanted a reputation because she was insecure.

Hannah screamed because her uncle raped her when she was twelve. Sadly, during my subsequent thirty-year career as a man dedicated to pursuing sexual intercourse, a percentage of women I've had sex with also have screamed during the act. Not out of pleasure but again, because of a bad uncle, father, husband, stranger, cousin, doctor or social worker. For this reason, disgusted by my own gender (for one of innumerable reasons), when the opportunity presented itself, I decided to avenge Hannah, but not just Hannah. Hannah stood for all women, not just the ones I'd fucked, but every woman who'd ever been raped, molested, harassed, abused or made to suffer at the hands of men.

*

Autofiction. Darina told me this publication is dedicated to 'autofiction', the narcissistic quicksand of literature. But she didn't want to know what was true and what wasn't, helpful for me in that I often have trouble distinguishing between the two.

When Ted Bundy was arrested after massacring a sorority house at Florida State University he denied it all. But Ted had a big ego and loved an audience. Orenthal James Simpson, long after being acquitted for having murdered Nicole Simpson Ronald Goldman, published a book called *If I Did It*. In it he describes how the murders would have been committed, if he'd done it (which of course he did), in the third person. Bundy, who the public often mistakenly thinks was charming and intelligent, when told that he was of interest to science, and that FBI profilers wanted to learn from him (feeding into his insatiable ego), began to provide specific details to dozens of the murders he'd been charged with, but did so in the third person…

"He would have chopped her head off, buried it a mile away from the body…then at night he would've come back, dug the head back up and masturbated into the skull. This is what he would have done. And the skull would be at mile marker 16, while the rest of the body, which would still be adorned in a flowered skirt and socks with little bows, the left breast bitten off…"

Once Bundy exhausted his last death penalty appeal, he switched to the first person. Perhaps OJ Simpson will switch to the first person on his deathbed and explain what he felt, seeing his estranged partner's head attached to her spinal column by just a handful of ligaments.

So in the spirit of autofiction I'll take advantage of all that this most dubious category of writing allows me, I will tell my revenge story in Ted Bundy pre-appeal exhaustion style. I do so in part because while I did serve the time handed down to me, minus two years for good behaviour, I'm uncertain of the statute of limitations on certain crimes in Canada, and my own culpability in what happened is murky and uncertain. I don't have the energy to spend weeks researching the Canadian legal system to find out which tense I can I write this in, so will later follow the lead of Bundy and Simpson, two champions of intellect, so that I can tell my story with complete accuracy and hot have to be concerned I may be asked to step aside by large and square-faced customs officers the next time I attempt to cross the border into the United States of America.

In 2005 I was thirty-five-years old and lived in a town called Smithers in northern British Columbia. The population of Smithers is divided into halves; First Nations people and cocaine loving, alcohol appreciative loggers. I never really fit in there but needed a place to go for a year. My life in Vancouver was slowly burning down and the best solution I had back then was, instead of attempting to put out the fire, to get as far away from it as possible. I worked for a private forestry company, skimming sections of old-growth trees that had been logged and spliced. I operated a machine that separated the bark from the wood like dead skin from a sunburn. Some of the trees were over two thousand years old, and the forest often felt haunted. The largest trees in the world grow in Northern British Columbia. I used to get quite sad when I was stripping a tree which had been quietly minding its own business since the birth of Christ.

There were two bars in Smithers. One was appropriately unwelcoming to white people, so I was forced to drink at the one that was not. I typically minded my own business and was methodical in my drinking, consuming six double Jim Beams with a single ice cube over the course of three hours. I spoke to only one person, Garnett, a man I'd later read in the newspaper had killed his own brother, with whom he'd been having consensual sex, high on crack, since the age of twelve. I made a grave error three months into my time in Smithers - I brought a book to the bar. From what I remember, it was *The Human Stain* by Philip Roth. Like in high school as in Smithers... reading a book exposed me to taunts of 'fag' and, its clever variant, 'faggot.' One particular idiot, who I later learned was named John, would not let it go, that I was reading a book. There are certain environments in which men congregate where literacy is nothing more than a sign to those who observe the reader that the reader thinks he is, 'better than you.' I did not then and do not today think I am better than anyone. Reading in that environment signifies only otherness, condescension, or as mentioned, homosexuality. John kept trying to goad me into fighting him with the following line,

"I'm gonna fucking kill you fag."

Sometimes he mixed it up,

"I'm gonna kick your ass fag. Let's go outside."

I've never enjoyed the idea of 'going outside' to settle an ambiguous beef with another man, because 'outside' is where violence happens.

John's friends, some of whom knew me enough to nod at me without disdain, but not with affection. They attempted to calm John down, tell him that I "wasn't worth it." I'd of course been doing nothing but quietly drinking and reading. After John first expressed his desire to cause me physical harm, I'd gone so far as to close my book to mollify him and correct the insult I'd apparently made. It did no good. I was wary of leaving the bar because John had other friends that were less discouraging of his desire to smash my face in, and I didn't want to find myself in a five on one type scenario. I figured John would drink himself into uselessness, or at least forget he wanted to fight me. This did not happen. Eventually the bar was empty save John and me. The owner had mistakenly kept it open past closing as a result of having passed out drunk himself. There were only four hours before everyone had to be up again and back amongst the doomed trees. I caught sight of John who was struggling to keep his head up with one hand and slipped out of the doors into the parking lot where my 1982 grey Subaru 4WD wagon was waiting for me, its backseat practically oozing homosexual reading material. As I approached the car I heard the word I'd often heard yelled at me way back when I'd been desperate to fuck Hannah,

"Hey, Fag."

Since the lot was empty, and I was the only one reading Philip Roth, I knew that fag was me.

I did my best to discourage John from fighting. I am six foot two, John was five and a half feet if he was an inch but possessed the prehistorically dominant musculo-skeletal structure of a man built for fighting other men. I did not feel confident. John kept coming towards me, and I kept backing up. Not out of cowardice, although I am a coward, but because I don't like violence, and also worried John might kill me. At a certain point we were a foot apart and it became evident I'd have no choice but to fight. This is one example of the utter stupidity of men. We had to fight, but of course we absolutely did not have to fight. John had puked slightly on his jacket and when he went to push me I was more concerned about vomit transfer than I was about physical injury, so dodged him, sending him to the ground. Embarrassed at having fallen down, John was angrier than ever. I was called fag numerous times. When he got to his feet and began to rush me I did something I'd only done once before at that point, I punched him as hard as I could directly in the face. He dropped like a cinder block from a third-floor balcony.

"Okay John, that's it," I said, "I don't wanna hurt you. Let me help you up."

John said nothing. I noticed he wasn't moving whatsoever. I felt relieved that I'd 'won' the fight, but also didn't want to leave him there unconscious in the parking lot. There was a chance he'd catch hypothermia or lose his job the next day for showing up late, or not at all. I crouched down and shook him, hoping he'd wake up. Nothing happened. I noticed blood in his left ear. This seemed negative. I put my forefinger on his neck to feel for a pulse and there was none. I put my ear next to his mouth (which stunk of high-beer content vomit and made me retch) and could feel no breath. After doing a few other things I'd seen on television, I realized John was dead. I'd killed him with a single blow to the head. This thing does happen from time to time, as in the case of Jakub Moczyk, a twenty-two-year-old boxer who died from a single punch during a match in 2017. My cousin Heather is deaf today after having suffered total hearing loss while competing in an Irish dance contest as a child. Either her brain was abnormally small or her skull abnormally large, but either way, the jarring movements of the Irish jig rattled her grey orb around her hard shell, obliterating her hearing. Brains are frangible things. Poor John, tough as an ox on the outside, was internally as delicate as a ballerina. I panicked, which to this day I view as reasonable. When I ran inside the bartender was still passed out, and there was no sign of anyone in the vicinity whatsoever. Hindsight being what it is, I really should have called the police. Dozens of people had witnessed John antagonizing me and had seen me persistently attempt to avoid fighting him. It would've been a simple case of self-defense, open and shut. But I panicked. There's a certain lack of justice in the more uncharted areas of the Pacific Northwest, a sort of hangover, extra-judicial Wild West mentality. Men may fight to the death over a woman, and since likely each of the say, five police officers covering that district would likely be related to one of the people involved in the crime, the typical results we expect from the justice system would likely not play out.

I've watched a lot of movies and television. I've seen innumerable scenes in interrogation rooms where people such as myself, readers of literature, are told what great wives we'll make for inmates named Bubba, Bubba 2, Big Rick or Fat Dwayne. I did not want to get raped in prison, and again, recognized the reasonableness of this thought as soon as it entered my mind. Passed around, watch your back in the yard, don't drop the soap, and not as a funny ironic thing you say to your partner in the shower. This was murder, the Big Show. Twenty to life, this sort of thing. Hundreds of scenes from entertainment media flashed through my mind in the two seconds it took me to make the most unwise decision of my life. I can remember the smell of the air as I grabbed a sleeping bag from my truck. It was the inimitable smell of slaughtered wood in an unpolluted autumn sky, tinged with the moisture of fog I felt with supra-intensity entering my nostrils. I pulled John's body (corpse) up to my truck, lay down my sleeping back and rolled him on top. Then I stuffed him inside, zipped it up and lifted him, with no small effort, into the backseat of my Subaru. This area of Smithers is all logging roads, many of which have been out of service for decades as they'd been denuded of usable tinder and now are dotted with young trees planted to replace their ancestors. I drove with my headlights off down a small logging road towards the Chalk River, then pulled down a secondary road that was more of a path through the forest. I tried to have some respect for John's corpse when removing it from the backseat, but found myself ungraceful, and he thudded ignobly onto the dewy ground. I kept hoping the sleeping bag would begin to seize, as if he were a stunned cat in a pillowcase about to be drowned suddenly sprung back to life. This did not happen. I had tire chains in the back which were sometimes necessary, as early as November, when snow began to fall in the high mountains long before it would touch the city streets in Vancouver. I wrapped them tightly around the sleeping bag John was 'big-sleeping' in. This was it. This was what a putative future biographer would call a 'turning point' in my life. I dragged my package towards the bank of the river, kicked it hard once to give John a chance to resurrect, and when he didn't, rolled him into the frigid water. The current was rather fast, and while I smoked a cigarette he floated away, momentarily becoming stuck on a fallen tree. He was not sinking, and this bothered me. I watched him drift further from sight, but he still remained afloat. Eventually he was gone. One part of me felt relieved while another began to churn deep from within a new kind of panic. I was the last one seen with John. I had in fact killed him, unintentionally or not, self-defensively or not. With my boot I tried to rub away the drag marks which just made a new, possibly more suspicious mark in the mud. Once I got my truck back onto the logging road I took off my shoes and socks, returned to the bank of the river and used my hands to wipe away the trail of my boot tread. It all just looked worse to me. Now it didn't look like a simple crime scene so much as a calculated attempt to cover up a crime scene. What would Philip Roth do flashed through my head. Write about it, I thought. Then I thought, "I don't even like Roth, honestly. He just puts out a book every year and I worry I'll seem remiss as an intellectual if I don't read each one. In reality I haven't liked anything he's done since *The Ghost Writer*."

I drove back to camp. Everyone was deep in their last hour of sleep. John's roommate was sleeping alone of course. I was wired. My roommate Clay hadn't heard me come in. I washed my hands and face, lay on the bed and waited for my alarm to go off.

"Well boys," I heard in the meal tent at breakfast, "the fuck if I know where John went. Anyone see him?"

I saw him. I knew where he was. I stuffed my mouth with seven pieces of bacon.

By one in the afternoon the cops were at our camp. In the back of their squad car I knew someone had snitched, likely one of John's Early Man allies, and mentioned that he and I had been going after each other in the bar. If it'd been anyone other than one of his Early Man allies, they would've reported that John was going after me, and I myself had kept trying to defuse the situation. Snitching was akin to blasphemy amongst the men I worked with, but I wasn't one of them, so the bullshit male honour code didn't apply. I wasn't even a man as they saw it.

The Smithers police department is small, like something from a movie where there's one dumb cop, one constantly harangued female secretary, and one aggressive cop. Three employees in total, each man inept, the secretary imprisoned in a building containing a small prison. Twice in my life I've been (mis)diagnosed as a sociopath. I have most of the primary symptoms:

Superficial charisma.

Lack of respect for authority.

Affectlessness.

Manipulativeness.

Impulsivity.

Engagement in Risky Behaviours.

Stunningly effective deceitfulness

What I don't have is a lack of empathy, evident in the fact that I worried John would catch hypothermia or lose his job, even though I had no reason to care whatsoever about his well-being.

The symptoms I have just happen to also be symptomatic of someone with Borderline Personality Disorder, or Post-Traumatic Stress Disorder, of which I have both. As a child it was urgently important that I develop the ability to charm my way out of situations. Like making my grandfather laugh so that the shovel he was about to bring down on my head would be dropped in the midst of his guffaws. Lack of respect for authority results from authority figures having caused me great suffering. Also, fuck authority and fuck the cops. Affectlessness is akin to dissociation. My interior world is so busy and overwhelming that were someone to observe me, I'd appear preoccupied and emotionless, staring at the wall while inside of me empires crumbled. Manipulativeness again was a skill I needed to develop to avoid danger. Impulsivity is the byproduct of trauma in that one becomes both addicted to dopamine and aloof about death. Engagement in risky behaviours, the same. Risky behaviours reward my dopamine receptors, which temporarily gives me pleasure. Risky behaviours also let me flirt with suicide without making a solid commitment. Deceitfulness again is a defective mechanism borne of trauma, in that lying was often the most effective way to avoid being abused.

I never set fires.

I never harmed animals.

I never pissed my pants after the age of ten unless I was wasted and the line for the bathroom at a party was too long. Even then I was more inclined to take my dick out and piss in a plant - lack of respect for authority.

It was my expertise with deceit and manipulation that kept me in the interview room instead of in a cell. Had I seen John and had we been arguing? Well, he'd been arguing with me, and I'd been doing my best to calm him down. Surely dozens of people can tell you that, officer. Yes I'd seen him last. He was terribly wasted. The bartender had passed out, it was getting cold and I wanted to get back to the camp. John had forgotten about wanting to fight me and was mumbling that he was, "sorry Erica, it meant nothing to me" while I took off his shoes and covered him with a blanket, leaving him tucked in and safe in a booth at the bar, which is where I last saw him before driving back to camp.

For every question I had an answer. I was unwaverable. I was certain. My answers to their questions never changed. I was not nervous or agitated. I was not sweating. I did not chain-smoke or ask too many questions. I offered my assistance but did not offer so much assistance that I fit a profile. The profile of the killer who assists in the search party. After four hours with Constable McEwan and Detective Barry I was told,

"Go back to work Brad. If we need anything we'll get in touch. My thinking is that John woke up drunk and confused and maybe wandered into the woods."

"That sounds possible," I said. I did not say, "Yeah, that sounds right." Because I needed to offer room for doubt, my own doubt. If someone accused of murder suggests that alternate explanations may be plausible, but not likely or certain, they appear to be neutral. Neutrality is one of numerous keys to reducing one's own suspiciousness.

Two weeks later, John's bloated corpse washed up on the bank of a creek attached to the Chalk river. That was my sleeping bag. Those were my tire chains. I was arrested. I plead my case. Witnesses came forward to support my side of the story, that John had antagonized me all night. I claimed self-defence. The pathologist reported that John had died from a blow to the head. One time in half a million she told the jury. Very rare, very rare indeed. Interference with a corpse, failure to report, manslaughter. Instead of facing the possibility of conviction for all three offences, I ended up taking a deal. Third degree manslaughter. I was sentenced to five years at Matsqui Penitentiary, where I'd be eligible for parole in three, contingent on good behaviour.

I did not bring any books with me to prison, nor did I ever check any out of the library.

*

Everything Brad had seen in movies and television about prisons proved to be accurate. People say that it's a cliche to say all cliches are true. At this point it's also cliche to say that it's cliche to say that all cliches are true.

But prison cliches, they're true.

Two things contributed most to Brad being released from prison unraped after serving three years of his sentence. One was the classic movie standby wherein, ironic considering his dispute with John, his literacy and way with words allowed him to help fellow inmates work on their appeals, and craft eloquent letters to their paramours on the outside. The second helpful thing was the protection of the Aryan Brotherhood. Brad was no racist, nor as it turns out, are seventy-five percent of the members of the Aryan Brotherhood inside penitentiaries. In fact the Brotherhood transacted most of its narcotic business inside the walls with black and First Nations prisoners. Brad would've had to start out as a skinhead's bitch to be allowed access to the lily-white sanctum had he not been crucial in assisting 'Killer Mike' in drafting his appeals. As in Smithers, so in prison, being a slight and unimposing man with a fondness for books and a tendency towards polysyllabic words, Brad was, to say the least, quite vulnerable.

Another prison cliche that proved true was the violent disdain inmates have for pedophiles. It was this cliche, after being transferred to a different cell six months into his bid, that put the idea of avenging Hannah into Brad's head.

Hannah had been very important to Brad, both before and after her death, and throughout the years he'd maintained a friendly relationship with her family. He'd been to her funeral, which was sparse and vaguely cursed due to the manner of her death, and ended up spending the night at her parent's house after the wake. Her mother Grace and her father Mark were both stunned to learn that Grace's brother Dante, the bad uncle, had raped Hannah when she was twelve. Understandably it was the central focus of her suicide note. Brad told Grace and Mark that Hannah revealed what happened to her way back when they were dating in high school. As a result, they viewed him as a source of unknown information about their dead daughter. When you lose a loved one what you hunger for most (other than their return) is information. You want to know their secrets, but you also want to know what their favourite song was, their favourite band and colour. You want to know what memories they most cherished. In short, you want to know absolutely everything you didn't know before, because you regret not having known, and you hope that perhaps one day in the future, your loved one might have shared with you these small parcels of information that together make up the whole of the dead.

Brad was transferred from his cell six months after arriving as a result of the coprophilic activity of his cellmate Teddy. Not only did he save his shit in rubber gloves to toss at guards, he also used it to paint rudimentary sketches on the walls, creating a perpetually shit redolent environment Brad found intolerable. Brad had become friendly with Cecilia, a guard, and she agreed to let him transfer to a more chill wing of the prison. There that he was paired with James Earl James (a very prison-sounding name), who was serving a life sentence without parole for the triple murder of three young men. A year into Brad's sentence James developed brain cancer. He was approaching seventy-five. He'd been inside Matsqui for fifty-one years and felt genuine remorse for the gruesome act he'd committed high on PCP. James hadn't quite found God in the penitentiary sense, but he'd become a spiritual man with a highly developed moral code. In typical inmate fashion he detested pedophiles, and in 1997 put eleven holes in a new prisoner who'd been convicted of molesting a dozen prepubescent, mentally handicapped children that his mother was fostering. He managed to survive the punctures made of a razor sharp toothbrush only to be tossed off a third floor railing two months later.

Brad knew Hannah's uncle's name was Dante, and he knew he still lived in British Columbia. Grace had told Brad in a letter three years previous to his incarceration that Dante was living in Surrey, a suburb of Vancouver, and that Mark had become obsessed with finding him and delivering 'real justice'. Grace had asked Brad to talk to Mark on the phone and he managed to talk him down, reminding him that while it would most certainly feel good in the moment, he'd be abandoning his family and ultimately would suffer far more than Dante after his inevitable arrest. Brad couldn't offer Mark either comfort or alternate solutions to his reasonable fury. Dante was protected by the statute of limitations, which infuriated all three of them. But now paired with James, Brad realized there was something he could do. It wouldn't be hard to find Dante. Besides Mark and Grace, Dante was likely the only other person in British Columbia with the last name Dankworth.

One night while playing blackjack before bed, Brad told James what'd happened to his high school girlfriend.

"She was only twelve James. I mean fuck, who does that. And it killed her, I mean literally--she committed suicide later on. Her funeral, Jesus, funerals like that you don't forget. I dunno, I really cared for Hannah. If she hadn't been so destroyed by her uncle I imagine we might've gotten married, had kids. I might not be here now. I think she's the only girl I've ever loved."

"This," James said, "this I can't abide. And he's out there today, so you know the motherfucker's still doing it. I wish I had any contacts left out there, but they're all dying like me these oldtimers. Either that or in jail. Suicides, OD's. None of us were meant for this rotten world."

Brad brought Hannah up at least once a week. He knew about the policy at Matsqui. Once James's cancer had metastasized to such an extent that the prison hospital couldn't provide for his needs, they'd grant him compassionate early release. That way he could end his life hooked to a morphine drip in a real hospital in the city. And he had a granddaughter, Elise. James had been a model prisoner outside of the time he shanked that short eyes, and even that, well, nobody particularly views that as bad behaviour. Two and half years into Brad's sentence, it was announced that James would in fact be granted early release. His body was nothing more than a playground for tumours, and his suffering was immense. He'd moan in his sleep like a beached whale and spend most of the clutching his stomach, where tumours were building condominiums in his intestines. The cancer was everywhere. The doctor's said that once he was out, James would only have a few weeks, a month at best. He'd be able to see his granddaughter, make peace with the world, and have a say in the design of his gravestone. Small gestures that meant a lot to a man who'd spent a half century behind bars. Brad was manipulative, charming, twice mistakenly diagnosed as a sociopath. He didn't even have to suggest the idea to James, he knew it'd come naturally, and then one day it did:

"Brad. Maybe this, I can redeem myself. Elise doesn't know me, and to be honest I don't think I'd want to see her. Up until now her life's been innocent and respectable. What does she need with meeting a murdering cancer ridden grandfather for the first time to say a meaningless goodbye? But this thing with Hannah and that fucking uncle. I'm not going to heaven junior, I know that much. But maybe there's a way I can secure a more comfortable seat in hell."

That was all it took. It was as if Brad had slipped the idea firmly into James' brain, and it fit as snugly as a sympathy card in an envelope. Two weeks before he was released Brad gave him Dante's name. There was an unexpected and happy surprise just days before James left - Cecilia, the guard who'd transferred Brad out of his shit cell, had been privy to their conversations about Hannah. She, like any prisoner, like anyone really, also hated pedophiles. Plus she'd made friends with James long before Brad showed up. The three of them got along. Sometimes she'd turn off the camera and pull a chair up outside the cell so all they could play cards. So it was that one day on their way back from lunch, Cecilia slipped a note into Brad's hand and put her index finger over her lips. The note said simply,

"Dante Dankworth. 11410 South Hoskins Avenue."

When James was released he took three things with him. A copy of The Sermon on the Mount, a picture of Etta James, and Cecilia's helpful note.

James was admitted to Mount Sinai Hospital's segregation unit immediately upon his release. Hospital guards are like rent-a-cops - they can't handle feces thrown at them by inmates, they can only handle inmates who sit in their own feces and hardly pose a physical threat. James took note of this immediately.

On his third day at Mount Sinai, he noticed that Adrian (a name he couldn't take seriously) would often take lunch breaks that lasted far longer than an hour. The nurses and doctors all thought James could die at any moment, a belief that was to his advantage. So on that third day, while Adrian stuffed his face at an Arby's opposite the hospital, James simply got out of bed, walked himself and his IV drip to the elevator, down one flight and out the front door. He unhooked himself and got into a waiting cab.

James asked to be taken to Vic's, a billiards club he knew to be immune to both gentrification and financial hardship as it had long been a clubhouse for the local branch of the Luchese family for whom he'd occasionally done 'favours'. Once inside he saw them, all like him but in dated suits. It was sad almost, the way criminals remain stuck in the fashion of their heyday. Any of these men out on the street would be subject to laughter from hip young people,, laughter that would instantly be silenced by the surprise of a ball peen hammer wielded by octogenarians pulverizing stylish knee bones. Two men inside recognized James and welcomed him in, mocked his pajamas and offered him cigars and drinks, both of which he accepted. There was a round of where've you beens and howsyall doings. But nothing had changed. Old men collecting increasingly slim envelopes and an old man with increasingly slim time on earth.

"I need a gun." James said to a man named Tony whose alcohol compromised nose was weighing down his face.

"Vito, go get a gun for Uncle James."

Vito, Uncle. If James knew more about the cliches wielded by mafia films he would've laughed, but he saw no irony in this world.

"What're you gonna do James?" a fat fuck named Fat Frank asked him.

"I'm out boys. I've gotta settle one thing before I walk into the woods and die."

"Good enough. Take what you want, just let Vito get you a new outfit and finish your drink."

"I don't know where there's clothes Uncle Frank," Vito said.

"They're on your fucking body you idiot. Strip and give them to our guest."

Vito disrobed, leaving on a pair of black silk boxer shorts. The clothes would've once been too small, but with James having lost so much weight recently, they fit perfectly. He picked a discrete Luger from the selection of guns offered to him, polished off his bourbon and a second, asked Fat Frank for five hundred bucks which he happily provided and headed out the front door.

That night James slept at Super 8 motel. None of the shows made sense. A bunch of fucking whiny idiots living in a house together, constantly filmed being whiny idiots was called Big Brother. A bunch of fruits dressing dumpy straight men with dumpy straight wives was called Queer Eye for the Straight Guy. All that made sense was Judge Judy, who he'd watched on the inside. She didn't put up with shit, called people idiots every five minutes, and generally seemed like the kinda woman James would've designated a great first wife.

In the morning he went to IHOP but found he had no appetite. He took a cab to 11410 South Hoskins Avenue in Burnaby which cost him seventy-five dollars. He gave the cabby his remaining four hundred to fuck off for two hours. James swore he wasn't gonna drive it anywhere, he was just hoping to surprise his grandson. The cabby did fuck off, and James sat (slumped) in the backseat, keeping his eyes glued to the front door while his hand sentimentally caressed the handgun. Some things change, but bullets and barrels and triggers rarely do. James was weak and had to bite the inside of his cheek enough to draw blood to stay awake. Forty-five minutes into his 'surveillance' he saw a piece of shit looking man walk out the front door of 1140 South Hoskins. The guy looked about his age, which seemed right according to what Brad'd told him. James opened the door of the taxi, cocked the gun and began to walk towards the figure exiting the house.

"Dante." James said.

"The fuck are you?" the man asked, verifying he was in fact Dante.

James said nothing. He held the gun behind his back and walked slowly towards Dante, who was frozen in place, curious to know who this old man in the Donny Brasco outfit was.

"What do you want"" Dante asked. James said nothing, just kept approaching.

Now within a foot of Dante, James revealed his pistol. He'd decided that Dante indeed had the appearance of a diddler. Guns do two things to people besides kill them - make them run or make them freeze. Dante froze.

As he was about to speak, pitifully hoping he could talk his way out of whatever beef this old man had with him, James quietly said,

"This is for Hannah," then shot Dante twice, once in the head and once in the chest.

Then he sat on the curb and waited for the cops to arrive.

MAN NEWLY RELEASED FROM PRISON ASSASSINATES MAN IN BROAD DAYLIGHT emblazoned the front page of the *Vancouver Province* the next morning.

James had offered no resistance to the cops. They'd been interviewing him for two hours. To the consternation of the detectives, each and every time they asked James why he'd killed Dante, he offered the same response.

"He had it coming."

These four words were the only ones James spoke. The cops looked for any connection between Dante Dankworth and James Earl James but could find nothing.

"James," they'd say. "We've talked to your warden, to your doctors. You've got a week left at most. Maybe this is something you wanna get off your chest so you can die with a clean conscience. Tell us what happened."

"He had it coming." was all they ever heard.

James felt something, but wasn't sure it was redemption. If you've never been redeemed, how can you know the feeling. If you've never been loved, how can you know what it means when someone tells you they love you. If you've never eaten lasagna, how can you even be sure lasagna's what you're eating?

The detectives, whose number had increased due to the bizarreness of the scenario, were treated to four new and different words from James, the last time they asked him yet again why'd he done it.

"Get me a Sprite."

This gave the cops hope. Maybe a Sprite would get the old man talking. Maybe he hadn't had a Sprite in a half century. One detective stayed in the interrogation room while another went to the vending machine. As four others watched behind a one-way mirror James, who'd always hated Sprite, closed his eyes, leaned left, fell off his chair and died.

RELEASED PRISONER TAKES THE MYSTERY OF HIS DAYLIGHT ASSASSINATION TO THE GRAVE read the headline of the *Vancouver Province* evening edition.

Brad was released from Matsqui three months after James helped him to do something he himself just wasn't capable of. Cecilia was a vault. She'd never utter a word to anyone. During the preceding three months detectives had come to interview him a half dozen times, but Brad told them James had never mentioned any Dante, that he'd hardly spoken at all. A man like this Brad told them, he's old school, he does his time, his time doesn't do him. We played cards, but other than that he was a monk. There was absolutely no way for law enforcement to connect James to Dante to Brad. "This is for

Hannah," had only been heard by Dante. Brad had dated a plethora of other women since the one he'd first lost his virginity to. He was golden, untouchable.

Each year on the anniversary of James' death, Brad would pay a homeless person fifty bucks to go buy a dozen roses and have a card inscribed with the following,

"Love from Hannah."

Once he got the flowers back, he'd then pay another homeless person fifty bucks to go leave them on James' grave.

While everyone's forgotten, no one is forgotten. One particular detective, stymied by the whole scenario, would go to James' gravesite every year or two and notice the bouquet. Whoever this Hannah was, he wasn't too interested in looking for her.

THIS IS WHAT I HAVE TO SHOW FOR LIFE

Darina Sikmashvili

I moved to a small town in the Midwest, devoid of friends and acquaintances, so that I might escape the impulse to create meaning from my time. I thought this self-imposed isolation seemed defiant and painful enough to merit a change.

Some recent morning I woke up and retrieved my phone. I was maybe looking at sunscreen, reading about the effects of the elements on aging skin. The atmosphere was roaring with pollutants, my face had stopped retaining moisture as it once had been able to, my complexion was wilting. The emotive face of my youth had brought early wrinkles and fine lines, a kind of punishment for living loudly, for opening my mouth, for laughing. I was beginning my slow descent down, I read. In a review, a woman raved about a drugstore serum that was life changing: I feel brighter, I feel a burden lifted. So much money down the drain but it's finally come to an end! Safe for daily use and best of all EASY. Light almond scent. I feel like me again. A phantom humiliation passed through me, like taking notice of lipstick on a stranger woman's teeth.

This took two hours of my morning. This morning my phone is off, away. I am writing by hand on crisp cream-colored paper. I am treating my attention with discipline, like a child in a dunce cap.

I then, naturally, got upset about my obsessing. Determined to make use of my wasted time, I requested to return a skincare product I found sitting on my kitchen table—a liquid meant to remove dead cells from your face—and was granted the refund promptly and told to keep it. I circled my apartment looking for what else I could dispose of; a small pile of bottles and fabrics accumulated quickly. I made a note to return them too, to donate them. What may for a moment have felt altruistic quickly turned into the desire to be rid of anything that reminded me of my poor habits. And everywhere I looked, I found them. I tried to calm down. Where was my sense of self control?

The radio in my bedroom was on, a program featuring a police officer who was heard screaming as rioters crushed his body with their greater agenda. There was first a description of the incident by a woman's voice, calculated, and then an audio clip from an interview with the officer; he described feeling, "well, this is it" and screamed ravenously not, he said, as a last-ditch effort to garner attention and help, but to proclaim his existence for the last time. Over his response, the radio station engineer overlaid the audio of the police officer's yell. His voice, an arrow, pierced through the din of protestors. His voice excavated him from the rubbles of near death. A cracked cheekbone, an aching shoulder.

I changed my clothes. It was 11:52am. I drew the blinds in my living room.

For an online exercise class which is mysteriously named The Class. It is an uncomfortable, aerobic experience lasting an hour. On the screen, the instructor wore a light grey unitard, the walls were painted grey and little light, all of which was overcast, was let in through a slit of long, grey curtains. A large candle encased in glass stood near the instructor, the only shift in an otherwise monochromatic color scheme. It was as if she was inside of a stone. The somber, fit woman with breastbones I could see pronounced through the spandex kept her voice clear and loud above the dance music. She was not a cheery person. During the warmup she spoke of pruning her plants, of how easily she had grown accustomed to ridding her life, periodically, of shit that drains this precious energy we are all here to foster while we, the class, hopped lightly in place with our eyes closed. I could not guess her age. She radiated discipline, a long-ago forged ability to regulate her desires in a matter so exact it must now have brought her pleasure sheerly to resist. The body adapts in impeccable ways to iron will. What the fuck did I know about this. When a morsel of kindness would come from her—and it always did with instructors of this kind, be it in word or gesture—I would savor the moment and feel myself deserving. Success by another's rubric suited me fine.

One exercise consisted of us squatting with spread legs planted firmly into the ground while our torso, arms, everything above the hips convulsed violently forward. I thought the instructor's intention was that we do this exercise in silence but soon I realized it was just the slow, quiet beginning of Tool's *Lateralus* that she put on. This meant we'd be doing a consistent exercise for nine plus minutes. For one summer in my adolescence, I took psychedelics near weekly and listened to Tool with a friend or a group of them. The first time we did this I had scared myself so intensely, wandered into a place so devoid of light, that my friend laid ice cubes across my chest, placed them in my palms, over my belly button, in hopes of shocking me back into my body. I laid on a rooftop with my eyes closed and my mouth parted for a long time, long enough to burn my face and arms, but my friend could not recall how long. Nor I, could then or now recall what came to me. Only the feeling of being emptied, of sensing the uselessness of my form, of my speech, which trapped itself in my memory.

Everything else, every interesting hallucination, texture, dissolved. I was hopeful the drugs, as they had been described by others, would make me more interesting, open me to the miracles of my surroundings, granulate the magnitude of each breath. But my journey was spent confronting my baseless existence. A shameful sense of my life as a smudge, a cosmetic inelegance on the delicate face of human history remained and followed me into adulthood, into this room.

To release further, we were to groan out our exhales. Bark them out. It burned my throat. I closed my eyes and worked so vigilantly to exorcise whatever was there that when I opened them, my legs buckled. When I stood up to alternate jogging in place with jumping jacks, Maynard James Keenan shouted, SPIRAL OUT, KEEP. GOING., while the instructor shouted, ARE YOU CHOOSING? ARE YOU IN CHARGE?

The closing exercise was categorized as a heart opener. I sat on my calves, folded efficiently, and spread my arms. They moved like doors on the hinges of my shoulders, fluttering first slowly then frantically. A bird testing the bones of her wings. My palms faced outward, the motion pulled the skin of my breastbone taut, pushed my chest forward. An image came to me, one I know intimately from a recurring dream: Two hands reach into my chest, past the skin, the muscle, the tissue, lace their fingers through the space between my ribs and crack me open, down my sternum, into two equal parts. The image is settingless unless white light is to count as a setting.

I returned to the living room—to the stale smelling living room on the second floor—and laid on my couch. It was the color of cooked oatmeal, a sallow grey I once admired for its minimalist flair and now, saw as repulsive. Sweat had long dried on my body, outside it had begun to snow and the wind blew it into the open kitchen window, a puddle had formed. There was *Lateralus* again, in my head, like a memory turned a corner. I turned it on and listened with my headphones. Maybe there was something in the song I was meant to talon into. I wanted to be urged to cross the line, some line, any line. I put it on again. Then once more. Again, with the volume all the way up. Here were the drums I remembered, the mania.

I lost count, but my lips were dry and when I finally stopped repeating the song, my arms and legs had bound up into one another as if I were burrowing into myself. Nothing came, only the stupidity of my efforts, magnified by the position I now found myself in.

I showered, shaved my legs, and put on a white cotton body suit, sweatpants and a sweatshirt. Before this was a series of oils I anointed myself with; I stood patiently in my bathroom, naked and shivering from the cold, waiting for one thing to absorb in order to proceed with applying another. My inner thighs, my pussy, smelled like lily of the valley. It was Christian Dior's favorite flower, the scent of his childhood, and he surrounded himself and his models, extensions of him, with the delicate little bells.

I had started seeing a man who worked on his computer at home near daily and did not mind being interrupted, so I would drive to him, usually unannounced, and this was not frowned upon. On my way I played *Lateralus* again and drove recklessly, too quickly, down a deserted street. The sun had come out; I'd look up at the sky and forget my speedometer, my foot relaxing on the gas pedal.

I was there to fuck him. Before going inside, I finished listening to *Lateralus*; the car had finally gotten warm. The man lived on a hill and the backyard he shared with a neighbor looked out at a baseball field and past that, a strip mall where I sometimes drove after our meetings for sundries and numb perusal. I didn't have the money for the person I wanted to really be, I thought to myself.

The man's neighbor, a man name Aaron, was outside smoking in the sun. I missed smoking. Quitting made me bitter, and I tried to convince myself that I could do things now, things that previously hadn't been near me: climb Mt. Fuji (it takes only one day, I'm told) and grow fond of running. Spend less money on beauty products, truly taste cantaloupe, examine the other places in my life where addiction reigned. No. Still I am happy I stopped, as it was difficult to overcome my impulses and in at least one area, I am succeeding.

I asked Aaron about his day and he answered by telling me he was enjoying his last cigarette. He had washed his clothes, all of them, save for the coat he had on, so he felt ready. Aaron is more interesting than I or my lover. He is a pyrographer; a wood burning of a mountain landscape, measuring six by eight feet, hangs in his apartment, originally intended for a woman who left him while they were on a road trip. He is legally blind; black spots float in his eyes and he can only see the periphery. To make his wood burnings, Aaron tilts his head in awkward positions and strains for hours. Migraines follow a good day of work and he smokes a lot of weed to counteract them, weary of Advil. He can't drive, he can't read books. Everywhere on a bicycle, listening to audio recordings of Brontë and Woolf.

He noticed that I cut my hair. What prompted my change? Nothing, I said. Well, it looks good. Do you think I look older, I asked. You look glowing, he said.

Before I had left my apartment I texted the man I was seeing to say I was eager to suck his cock. He responded that he would draw the blinds. I thought it was a good response, procedural and succumbing.

I'm not native to the English language, which is the language I know best. Still, I frequently second-guess my instincts and refer to grammar books, rearrange the words like color schemes in a sentence. My impulse is to put the predicate before the subject, so fond am I of the opportunity to create exclamation, to declare.

Now comes the fun. (transposed order)
The fun comes now. (normal order)
In such a sentence, either is possible and the writer has her choice. Except in sexting, where the normal order, the one a native English speaker would intuit, is preferred:

I am eager to suck your cock. (normal order)
Your cock I am eager to suck. (transposed order)
Here, the choice is clear. The ear wants to meet the subject first; the cock must follow, not lead. In a sentence as giving as my sext, as generous, I remain the subject.

I went into the man's house and saw that he had drawn the blinds in the living room. Recently the radiator in his apartment stopped working, and everywhere were plugged in electric heaters, emitting small pockets of heat. I walked into his bedroom where he warned I would be even colder, but he followed me and drew the blinds there. Now, shy of the kitchen, where a monstera plant thrived in a sliver of sun, the apartment took on the stale color of stifled daylight.

Do you know: my monstera plant had been nearing death all winter, though my doting was diligent and my watering, too.

We had sex. I kept the body suit on. He liked it, he said, how exciting. I made no mention of Tool's *Lateralus*, but it was in the room with us. Before I left for the man's house, I listened to it one last time with my headphones on. I turned the volume up and sensed the physical reaction I'd had those years ago, tripping: the drummer, Danny Carey, created a sort of rhythm which transferred the trembling in the music to a trembling in the ears to a trembling in the chest. There's a gathered fear to the sound, a persistent and pervasive technique that I imagined, in my ignorance of the medium, as having to do with time and measure. My body on the couch felt like a plate that would soon crack.

There is determinism in afternoon sex. The day had begun and it will continue, this activity exists in the center. I wanted to have sex because my morning had gone poorly, because my collarbones smelled of an emotional aromatherapy oil blend meant to promote peace and ward off disquiet, because sex is conclusive. We came.

The man made us tea and bagels. We discussed his work project on the floor near his couch, surrounded by a semicircle of electric heaters; he pronounced his goals clearly and simply. I worried he might ask about my morning and force me to declare my failures, but instead the man convinced me to stay for a half-hour and watch an episode of a television show he had recently gotten into, *Cowboy Bebop*. I was surprised to discover this activity felt the most self-indulgent to me that day.

The episode was about the character, Faye, a relentlessly sexualized and aggressive woman with a gambling addiction, desperate to learn about her past. Many of us struggle with our identity in a kind of grandiose, existential sense. Faye has no memory of herself. Surely when this is the case, what you know, the little self-knowledge you possess, seems imperative to your daily function. When the man turned to me and asked what was the matter, I could only zip my sweatshirt up, cover my head with the hood.

The smallest unit of writing is not the word, it is the intention.

I drove home in silence but opened the windows so I could hear the birds at the red lights. That day, I'd had six different instances during which I wanted to be intoxicated.

Cocaine.

Cold white wine.

Home, on my couch in the dying daylight, anti-aging again. The sun was bad and good. When I thought about my face, I could not imagine what I wanted to fix. I had no language for ailments, but the texture of change throbbed in me.

Because of this pervasive goal of physical wellbeing, I practiced yoga for half-hour in my bedroom lit by a single salt lamp. There were spine stretches, the instructor was a comforting woman who referred to us, the people watching her on a screen, as her dear friends. Take care, dear friends. Tread kindly on yourself. There will be less to undo this way.

Before I turned on this practice I stripped out of my lingerie and it lay on the edge of my bed, tangled up like a costume. My eyes darted in the direction of that person, now gone, while the instructor reminded me to soften my shoulders.

I drank a glass of water after fighting the urge to find a long blue wool coat on the internet. I said to myself that if I found the thought a second time, some days later, I could entertain it. My wants are swift and frequent and trifling. I find the relics of another's desires in my closet, on my vanity, my bookshelf.

If you would please just sit still, I said. If you would please just sit here with what you have. It was night. I reapplied deodorant and went to see a friend down the street, a woman I met recently at the grocery store. She drank cold white wine and I, cardamon tea. Her apartment walls were covered in elaborate leather wallpaper. The house was once a stately hotel. This wallpaper was not something I could have imagined in existence, let alone knew to desire. I had visited her apartment three times by then and each time—while she poured us tea or prepared something in the kitchen—ran my fingers across the wall. A blindfolded person touching the skin of an elephant, that is what I think of.

This woman is a great comfort to me. Visiting her that evening, I knew that like sex in the afternoon and yoga and neroli essential oil, I was aiming at self-soothing. My morning had been wasteful and I, a tantrum of a person, I felt my life wasteful as well. A kitchen sink full of dirty dishes, accruing more and more, stinking intensely of itself.

We spoke about her painting project. She too had had little success that morning, although from her account I argued otherwise. She had set out, in desperation, to draw from life, and chose a tall stand-alone radiator in the corner of her living room. After an hour or so of contours, she felt foolish and stopped. This is what I have to show for life? she laughed.

No, I said, and recalled a quote from the poet, Rilke, about what one must do for the sake of a few lines. She was polite and smiled in agreement, but I knew this was for my benefit only. With this friend I had previously fallen into wells: long, breathless discussions about suffering and our proclivity for it. We treated the conversation seriously, examined it like a logic problem; we'd ask one another, what do you think this comes from? We'd turn the ugly organ this way or that, a defunct heart on a surgery table, a greying lung. It felt beautiful to share this with someone, really. But each time I'd return home and feel as if I had exercised a muscle unfit for such strain.

She had, since I last visited, put cream linen curtains up in her living room. A huge window that previously exposed her (living in a fishbowl, she termed it) now provided elegant privacy. I noted to myself how much I must have liked being watched, so indifferent was I to her big open window and my lover's small, eye-level windows. What could they see, the few who would bother to look, that they wouldn't find in themselves? Two women talking, the sordid work of sex.

We spoke until ten.

I returned home and looked up a skincare product I saw in my friend's bathroom, a serum made from royal fern. Ferns are resilient and have been here longer than us and our problems. They lived at the bottom of the ocean. They adapted and sprouted on land. Monks in China boil the leaves and drink the elixir for its antioxidant properties. It made sense for one German dermatologist to add the sturdy shrub to a skincare line dedicated to combating signs of aging. The serum costs over one hundred dollars, the fern grows unadorned in backyards across Asian and Europe.

Here is a terminal sentence: I am aging. I want to know when the fat of my breasts will spoil, soften, tire. I want to know when men are going to stop darting up from their side of the aisle to assess me, some part of me, however little of me. When I will be discarded from their line of sight. I want to know when I am going to stop feeling like you and you and you want to fuck me. When I will stop flittering across the changing screen of someone's brain when they remember me, those days ago, pumping gas, sorting through citrus. It is coming to an end, my vanity is expiring, shriveling into indifference. The sugar of my lip balm sits too sweetly on my mouth; the sheen, now gaudy.

The radio was on. It was on nearly always on to keep me company. It was a voice. I have many times laid beside it and listened, like listening to changing waves: the bloodcurdling news and the music and the reviews and the comedy of children interpreting life. Tonight, on a program I listened to a man read missed connection letters and personal ads. People called in on the station's private line and were connected to one another, the host functioning like a switchboard operator. There were no commercials except for a few love songs. It felt like civic duty, this program.

I had a glass of water and an arugula salad with pine nuts, lemon, and parmesan, it was nearly midnight. I laid in bed, and thought, the way one might push the button to shut the elevator doors, push and push and push, why it is that we are eager to go where no one has been? What is it about transcending ourselves that appeals so much to us? Tomorrow was rushing in and I would wake up here, no closer, no further away. The skin still greying, the eyes gulping blind light, and nothing quite enough, quite close enough.

My therapist asked me some weeks back, earnestly—she's a not a very humorous woman—if it provided me motivation and comfort to generate difficulty and then wade through it. I felt helpless and embarrassed when I admitted in her office that suffering, endless and unnecessary, was what provided me with the only evidence of being alive. How pitiful, she said, and apologized immediately after.

NAMING THINGS

Aiden Arata

When another Ewan comes into my life, I worry it's my death drive.

"It's exposure therapy," says my therapist.

"I don't need to fuck an Ewan," I say. Under the trickle of the water filter there's buzzing, a power strip behind an appliance somewhere that needs to be reset.

"No one needs to fuck an Ewan." She sounds bored. I'm a little in love with her. Her computer camera faces some sort of music nook, and while she's explaining attachment disorders, I study the keyboard behind her, try to read the titles on her sheet music. Under the keyboard there's a small round bed for a pet I've never seen. The depth of field becomes an allegory for the depth of the subject—a reminder that I'll never know her. She gives curt, bitchy advice and I only follow it half the time, but I keep coming back.

"I'm worried about the turtles," I tell my therapist, because I want to change the subject, and I am. In the half-full aquarium on the kitchen table, one is basking under the red ring of a heat lamp. The other is swimming toward me, unaware of its barrier, beating its little webbed paws against the glass. My therapist says something, and I don't catch it, and we're at time, so I Venmo her, close my computer, and pack a bowl.

It's early December, after fire season but before the one week of rain, and all the wet has been sucked out of the air. I keep buying limes for some abstract future guacamole and then forgetting about them in the lidless Tupperware I use as a fruit basket, and weeks later I find them shrunken and hollow. Every day I wake up and my eyes are burning.

If you believe in getting high and dabbling in YouTube science, like I do, then you probably believe in multiverses. Mystical Space YouTube is disconcertingly proximate to Reptilian Overlord YouTube; I have to be mindful not to consume anything that would tilt my algorithm towards Nazism or suggest that powerful aliens actually care about something as trivial as the acquisition of capital. I am pulled, however, to twin suns and dying stars, quantum theory over a binaural beat.

I'd been on the couch in the dark, stoned, when I got the notification. The lights from the turtle tank were playing out on the far wall like a bad hand. On my screen, a feathered arrow shot backwards from a CGI target into the bow of a stock photo archer. There's an idea that alternate cosmos connect with ours, like many buds on a branch; each blooms outwards, or else it atrophies and doesn't. Our universe bloomed, is blooming. Sometimes things grow and collide. So it makes sense that five months ago Harry went on a two-week trip home to Montreal; and four months and two weeks ago there was a problem at the border, a clerical oversight, and he hasn't come home. It makes sense that the turtles' entire reality is contained by thin panes of glass, and outside that is death and chaos. And it makes sense that I had just been followed on Instagram by someone named Ewan, when a year ago (334 days) an Ewan—the only other Ewan in Los Angeles, the only Ewan I'd ever known—had sexually assaulted me.

The notification was six hours ago. I'm on the couch again, stoned again. After therapy, I had taken a break to pull two pieces of wheat bread from what Sprouts optimistically labels a "bachelor loaf" and heat them in a pan with a pat of oily butter, because I don't have a toaster. I sat at the kitchen table next to the turtles, smeared on more butter, and applied to jobs.

I used to be a television assistant. I had my own office on the lot and a clunky desk phone I couldn't work. I reported to a sharp-cheek-boned fitness enthusiast who wouldn't let me sit in on meetings but instead would have me compile lists of possible restaurants for her family to eat in when they went on vacation, or potential cold case episodic ideas, or potential Valentine's Day gifts for her husband, whom she told me she wanted to fuck on her shabby chic direct-to-consumer office couch as I was assembling it. Her father had been a pioneer of the 5pm murder mystery, leaving her a three-story house in Griffith Park and a spot in the room at a smattering of network dramas.

Once, over coffee, she had leaned conspiratorially across our table. "I know it's wrong, but"—a short laugh—"sometimes I think, why *not* Me Too?"

She sipped her latte and I sipped mine. I wasn't sure if the question was rhetorical, or if this was a trick, or the opening to a conversation about nepotism. I smiled, and she smiled back.

"The secret is, I don't need anything from anyone," she said.

By the end of my tenure, I'd lost my pleaser sheen. I was warm but dull, like an Edison bulb. I couldn't roll calls. I accidentally overstayed on a conference call, and realized that she was using the exercises she assigned me as original episode ideas. Ultimately, I was fired for failing to procure a high enough resale price from a West Hollywood consignment boutique on my boss' spitty designer baby clothes.

In addition to your resume, the job site requires that you answer company culture quiz questions like: *If I've worked an eight-hour shift and my manager asks me to stay on an additional shift, I feel: a) Invigorated; b) Resentful.* It's unclear whether they want obsequiousness or honesty in an employee; I opt for obsequiousness—*I would never schedule a doctor's appointment during business hours*—but I also haven't gotten any interviews. I've been subsidizing my unemployment with the occasional under-the-tax-bracket social media gig, ghostwriting memes for a regional chain of fast-casual pizza parlors and a third-tier mail order mattress startup. The work is inconsistent and the pay is comically low, and trawling Twitter for new joke formats is unexpectedly draining. I tweak my cover letters for yet another marketing position with an unlisted salary and wonder if my boss has the ability to blacklist me in industries other than her own.

I'm thinking about parallel universes, and the second Ewan. I pull up his profile. Most of his posts are screenshotted praise for the power of anarchist collectivism. Behind the flash of a mirror selfie, he has the long limbs and soft middle of a spider, a body shape I associate with the early effects of alcoholism.

I'd flicked through an Instagram infographic on reparenting… today? I can't remember—but maybe the same thing is possible for sexual trauma. A surrogate, a do-over in which I make better, different choices, or a universe in which I don't have to. The flush I feel looking at him could be similar to a crush. The prickle of hives creeping up my neck. Both Ewans have cats. Both Ewans have a slight lazy eye, but this one wears glasses. This Ewan claims to be a writer instead of claiming to be a comedian. His hair is darker, wavier. We have mutual friends, from New York and LA, from being pithy online. I list the differences out loud. I count to six while breathing in, and six while breathing out. I tap away from him, to a video of a mini horse playing with big horses.

Maybe I could trick him into saying sorry to me. Like I could choreograph it so he knocked my phone in some water, or something.

I go to my inbox, open a new message, type "what do i want from you" and then hold down the back button, horrified. It's incredible what we're capable of, how you could just write something embarrassing or cruel or insane and the words look like any other speck in the zettabytes of data in the world. The mini horse taunts the big ones, pixels blinking around, twisting my heart.

The day he got the turtles, Harry looked up turtle facts on our way home from Chinatown as I sped up the 110 Parkway. The plastic crate was on his lap and he was trying hard not to slosh them around. Red eared sliders live like 30 years, apparently, and grow up to 12 inches long. I'd been the one who wanted to go to Chinatown, I'd wanted boba and a phone case. I love all creatures in the universe. I'd had a few sliders growing up, and some hamsters that were indifferent to me, twitchy little pom poms that died of silent heart attacks in the middle of the night and you didn't even know until morning. No suffering but yours.

I spent the night before Harry left for Montreal walking around my apartment, picking up his sweatshirts and holding them up in front of him.

"This one?"

"I don't need it," he said.

"You said it's freezing."

Harry ended up packing two and leaving one, until the visa thing, and now I have five boxes of his clothes under my kitchen table.

Harry has the animated gesticulation and the humble slouch of a graphic designer, which he is, and the wide, placid face of a philosopher. He transfers money for the turtles' food and mine. He calls the turtles Phoenix and Pokey, but I don't know which is which, so I always refer to them collectively. Harry says that he understands that my anxiety is also a kind of care.

"Are you gonna get fucked again soon?" The phone is on speaker and I'm holding it out in front of me and the dark screen counts the seconds. My apartment smells a little like krill and a little like grease, because I keep getting stoned and ordering Popeyes Family Feasts and then freezing and reheating the leftover tenders all week.

The night before Harry left, we watched *SVU* and I made a dating profile. I asked him to pick the photos. We made out even though the episode was a graphic one. We stopped making out and went back to our phones and fell asleep to more *SVU*, then woke up and moved to the bed and slept more. Harry got up early, while I was still sleeping, and then he was gone.

"I don't know," I say. "Do you want me to?"

"Yeah," he says, his voice charged with desire and satellite transmission. "I want that."

I can't handle the smell. I walk out to my little porch of withered succulents and look around the brown yard. Beyond the grass is a low cement wall, a school parking lot and a two-story apartment building that was re-zoned as offices in the last gentrification wave and is now called the Sky Business Center. Across the street, there's singing from the Pentecostal Church. I bet they're totally getting off on the slow apocalypse. They even have a saxophone. It's a busy street, but Harry and I used to stuff our coat pockets with cans of Tecate and go around the corner to the tracks of the rarely functioning new metro, where it was quiet except for the occasional dog throwing itself against a chain link fence. We'd sip our beers and just walk around, pointing out plants we would put in future gardens.

"Did I shower when you were here?" I ask. I can't remember when I stopped. Harry says I did, that I always smelled good anyway. There's a hardware store on the corner that sells flowers and coconuts and once he went there for wood stain and brought me back a pink stuffed bunny. I crane my neck and look out into the flat purple night, stars and satellites. My phone vibrates. Ewan. A message.

Harry asks about the couple. The couple is a long-haired art guy and a tall girl with a slight gap tooth and a stoner's drawl. Portland transplants, according to the dating app. She's in e-commerce, which I think means she has a Depop, and he's in props, and for the last two weeks I've been sending them nudes. In return they send me descriptions of how they fuck while thinking about me, and I screenshot the sexts and send them to Harry, who masturbates to them. It's a whole economy. I have an iPhone tripod with a ring light that glints off my glasses. I unscrew my regular ceiling lightbulb and insert a pink one, and I shower and dress and put on makeup and push aside my laundry and unread books and empty ZzzQuil blister packs and lean forward, just a little, pushing my tits together, keeping my face out of frame. I'll take dozens and then swipe through them critically, studying these facsimiles of my cellulite or my underchin until I find the one or two that portray casual perfection. I hardly ever feel sexy after.

Harry and I talk about petty internet drama, two people we find annoying who apparently also hate each other. I walk out into the yard, not going anywhere, and turn the other way so I can see the San Gabriel mountains looming in the dark. Above them, each star is a loaded gun, and when I look at them I'm staring down the barrel of the future.

I look down again, find my inbox. The message is a reply to a story I'd posted, an eight-second video of the turtles in their primordial red expanse: "cute!" The air is still. Harry is still talking, blessedly, and I make noises where I feel I should. I know Ewan means the turtles, but it's also possible that he doesn't. I double-tap the message and close Instagram and tell Harry I need to wash my hair.

In the shower, I go to my profile and try to pretend I'm seeing it as Ewan. He'd been introduced to my humanity through my internet presence, which was unfortunate—the clubby lighting and the self-deprecation, the insular jokes with two-week half-lives. In some ways this endless feed is the more alive than my real life, but it's less human. I'm popular online, despite being only medium hot and medium funny. Or maybe because of those things. I have to feign interest when the Gen X marketing manager at the mattress startup pitches aspirational content and influencer deals, as if we aren't living in an economy of relatability. Ego is flat, like a mirror. In medieval texts a nun gets locked in a tower and has visions of the soul, and she says it's an orb with eyes in every direction. I don't think I've ever seen one, but I guess I'm seeing out of one all the time.

I check the dating app, where I don't respond to a smattering of dick pics, and then Instagram. A stranger says I look like a whale and need a nose job. I block them and look at Ewan's profile again, scrolling back to when he was thin and clean shaven. He seems to have been in the extended network of Brooklyn-to-LA creatives for a while, lurking in the periphery of my social reach at the Cha Cha Lounge or in a friend of a friend's story of a day at the beach. He was like a planet completing a long transit, orbiting back to me from the void of wherever people went when I wasn't thinking about them. I return to my messages. I wonder if he's seen my react, though even if he had, it wasn't exactly conducive to conversation. Maybe it had been cold and weird. I write him, "i'm bored," and send it.

I take a canted photo of my ass, open it in Facetune to smooth my thighs, and send it to the couple. I wash with rose scented Dr. Bronner's, shave one leg and give up on the second when the water starts to run cold. In my room, I send the horse video to Harry, who immediately love reacts it. While he's typing a response, I put the phone down and take the little plastic terrarium out from under the sink and fill it with an inch of tap water. I set it next to the big tank, where the turtles are basking under their special lamp that gives them some vitamin my windowless back unit living room can't provide.

I count droplets of water softener out into the plastic tank and dust the water with their foul smelling food pellets. The turtles are smart enough to slip off their floating foam island and paddle up to the glass when I bring out the feeding tank, but dumb enough to scramble away when I try to transport them there. I guess it's actually a sign of intelligence, in that it's about survival. Rabbits have a survival thing where you can hypnotize them—turn them on their backs and they go limp and docile, and you can pet them and they're perfectly still. You can tell people they love it. It's a glitch. They think they're about to die. I wish there was one word for that.

The turtles huddle in their overpriced rock hideaway. I hold my breath and keep my hand perfectly still in the vitamin-rich shit water until they come out and swim around me, forgetting I was ever not part of the environment.

They've gotten bigger. It's not even legal to sell baby sliders, because they're an invasive species and so prone to carrying salmonella, but when you buy them, you're actually just buying the cage. Our cage was twelve dollars and had plastic plants and a plastic crystal lotus glue-gunned to the inside. They'd been improbably tiny, barely silver dollar-sized. One was on the other's back, trying to climb out of their small world and into the big one, the crowded cart of plastic fans and knockoff Supreme sunglasses. Harry had said they were working together, and we watched them for a while before heading to the car. We made it to the flashing hand at the corner before turning around.

As I watch them snap at their pellets, I think, when Harry left they were just longer than my pinky, and now they're nearly flush with the palm of my hand. Their shells are a sacred geometry of infinite yellow whorls. One has a fresh welt on its leg, given to it by the other one. The internet says you need ten gallons of water for every inch of turtle, though Harry says you actually don't.

I don't tell him I've been thinking about the future. I've been looking into turtle rescues. There's no point, no one takes sliders anyway. When I was a kid and one of ours outgrew its fish tank, my mom would put it in her purse and take us to the Huntington, an Illuminati-esque private botanical garden whose oil baron founders were buried on the property in a marble mausoleum in an orange grove.

"Turtle paradise!" my mom would say, leading us past the blowsy rose gardens and the tropical plants. When we got to the lily ponds, she'd look around and then, if no one was watching, unceremoniously chuck the turtle into the water. We'd watch a swirl of little bubbles rise and wait for the turtle to come up, until the pond became still again and it didn't. My mom would take us to look at the Japanese bonsai trees and then take us home.

I looked up "pond release" in my rehoming research, only to learn that despite the red eared slider's prowess as an invasive species, the chances of them acclimating to a foreign biome were grim. Their only survival tactic was to decimate the ecosystem they'd just entered.

I press the lock button on my phone. No notifications. I wash my hands and half my dishes while listening to a podcast on manifestation, and then I scoop the turtles out of their little tank and put them back in the big tank. I dump the wastewater down the toilet, rinse the tank, and scrub my hands. I find a notebook among the detritus on my desk and I write Ewan over and over again, like a deranged sixth grader. It feels fucking terrible, hot shame chasing my hand across the page, so I write faster, the lines growing lopsided and butting into one another. It feels like sitting in a car's passenger seat while the driver accelerates into a wall. A collision— and suddenly it feels ridiculous, my fear boiling into vapor. Nothing's happening. I think about how life's only purpose could be to fill a cage, a cage that has value.

I check my messages again before bed. Ewan hasn't seen mine, unless he turned off his data and then checked the message and then turned it back on again, which would be psychopathic. But he has a new story—him and his cat, which appears to be the six-toed Hemingway kind, watching the TV show about the amnesiac flight attendant accused of murder. His bed is unmade, and I wonder how firm his mattress is. I wonder how he kisses, close-lipped or wet. I'm slightly better looking than him, I think, and more popular online. He might know this, and look at me with reverence, if I ever let him look at me. He might hook his hand around the back of my neck, pulling my hair very gently, and ask me what I like. I don't feel joy, but I feel desperation, which feels so, so close. I message him, "what are you doing tomorrow night."

For a while I was seeing an experimental therapist, a willowy blonde with the biggest diamond engagement ring I'd ever seen and a practice in a two-story Craftsman office park in Pasadena. The waiting room was always full of women like me; we'd flash strained smiles at each other and pretend to read Psychology Today. When it was my turn, she sat on a dove gray sofa and I sat in a cloud blue chair a few feet away from her and she spritzed her hands with lavender hand sanitizer. She ran her fingers over my face, my shoulders, my palms, while I told her about what had happened, reciting the details over and over. The stroking was supposed to rewire my neural networks, return my amygdala to factory settings.

Sometimes instead of what happened, I just said what I felt about it. Fear. Anger. Rage. Rage. Rage. I think I was supposed to exorcise the feeling that way, drawing it to the surface like a splinter. It felt more like a summoning. I repeated each word until it was a dumb abstraction, clunky in my mouth, until I cried and drooled over it and my therapist pet my face one last time and said the session was over. I paid $150 and left and ideated about flinging myself off the redwood second-floor balcony. I told the therapist I'd started crying in my dreams, and she told me to come more often.

I plug my charging cord into my phone and set it face-down on the pillow next to me. I roll onto my back, close my eyes, and am struck with a vision of flushing a turtle down the toilet with the wastewater. The tiny shell slipping from one body of water to the other, spinning out, gone forever. I roll out of bed and lumber into the living room, where I startle both turtles and they skid off their floating island.

I climb back into bed and name a type of food for every letter in the alphabet, twice, until my heartbeat slows. If I think anything else before I fall asleep, I don't remember.

I wake up to a text from Harry (a cringe tweet from a mid-2000s emo frontman) and a few DMs from strangers I talk to sometimes on the internet (mostly nice things, shared content and heart eye emojis). It's early, I think, until I realize it's after one.

He read the message. He didn't reply.

I make spaghetti with jarred vodka sauce and eat it while scrolling Twitter, feeling unfillable. I call Harry.

"The turtles are getting big," I tell Harry. He waits for me to go on, and I swallow, looking around the room. "Online it says they get territorial, when they don't have enough room."

Harry insists that the tank is twenty gallons while I look at the sticker on the side that says ten. He says the pet store got the sticker wrong. Animals fight sometimes, they work it out, he says. He's coming back soon, he's working on it, where's my patience, it's not his fault. I say okay. I hang up and wonder what to do with my day. Blissfully, it's already past three.

Without Harry or a job or any money, I spend most of my time on walks. Christmas lawn ornaments inflate of their own accord, possessed. I roll a sloppy joint and drive to Alhambra or Altadena or Glendale and walk around watching Santas rise. It's an auspicious time, my Saturn docking into its return, the north node traveling through my sign. Mars and Venus have been visible in the sky since June.

I choose La Cañada, flicking back and forth between my maps app and my messages all the way up the 210, like I'm tuning a dial to find an elusive station. Static—no new messages. Spanish Colonial Revival mini malls roll into sprawling Mid-century estates, the kind beautiful housewives once ate Valium in, and finally Angeles Forest, walnut and bigcone firs, metallic-smelling dirt and great, unknowable canyons.

I park on an empty street and get out, shoving my phone in my pocket. I light a joint, striking the empty air around me into flame.

I don't know why I try to push my humanity on people. Exteriorizing my interiority has always been an obsession, even before I was extremely online. To achieve this feels so elusive, like trying to tell someone an important dream you had, only to realize halfway through the story that it doesn't make sense and they don't care; the value of the vision is so intrinsic and slippery that when you try to say it, it's just a series of useless clauses.

I stroll what feels like miles, nodding hello at the occasional gardener or dog walker, tripping out on my own loneliness. I think about what my old boss is doing, and I send an intention into the universe that her children grow up to hate her. I consider walking up into the mountains. I put my phone on airplane mode so I can't look at it. I look at Christmas lights. I walk until I notice the same neighborhood patrol car passing me for the third time, saying nothing, but saying a lot.

Back in the lowlands I park behind a liquor store, wanting a seltzer. The lot is empty except for two girls in their late teens sitting on a parking block, passing their phones back and forth.

"Ma'am?" one stands up when I pass them. She's wearing a crop top I'm pretty sure I almost bought from Brandy Melville. Her friend sits, leaning away, shy or wary of me. "If we give you money can you buy us a Four Loko?"

My stoned synapses try to process the request, assess the possibility that the girls are undercover agents. I can't imagine that cops have much else to do in La Cañada. I imagine the girls cuffing me, taking away my phone, setting bail. Maybe a local news story about how I'm an enabling deviant that will follow me around on the internet forever.

"Sorry," I say. "I can't."

"Yeah, sorry, never mind," the girl mutters, and her friend stands, and they walk across the lot away from me.

I regret it before I make it to the door chime. I'd been a bitch, and an uncool one at that. They were too well behaved to have their own alcohol plug. They were probably going to get tipsy by one of their parents' pools, wander the neighborhood feeling powerful and free, and knock over someone's lawn reindeer. I wonder if they'll still be outside when I come out, or if I shamed them away. I couldn't explicitly provide them with alcohol—but if I bought a few cans, put them down in the parking lot, and conveniently forgot about them? I'm annoyed at my paranoiac bud brain, jumping to unreasonable conclusions instead of internalizing the information in front of me. Actually, I realize, I think like this all the time—picking up information only after the event, like I'm watching the news channel of my own life instead of living it.

I agonize over the flavors, ultimately choosing one Peach and one Blue Razz. I grab them, turn away, then turn back and take a second Peach for myself.

I walk out of the market, fiddling with the thumbwheel of my lighter, around back and into the shy girl's fist as she punches me in the face, a universe blooming, a burn from the plastic bag pulling where I'd twirled it around my fingers and their soft, even footfalls across the asphalt.

I step out of my clothes in the living room and throw them by the door. The girls took my Four Loko along with my wallet, so my choices are water or a three-day-old Popeyes soda fountain Diet Coke. I pull one of Harry's sweatshirts out of the box, put it on and sip the Diet Coke as I call him.

"I just fucked the couple," I say.

His breath catches. "Did you really?"

"Yeah," I say, "and I fucking loved it."

I've never understood destinations. Like I could be in the yard with my friends, having a nice time, and I'd be itching to go to a bar and spend all my money and smile at strangers. Then we'd get to the bar and I'd be looking outside every time the door opened, fidgeting with a napkin until I could ask about the afters. Some people seem to get one place and stay there and that's it, like there's some gravitational force that doesn't apply to me, no inertia to stop me from rocketing off the edge of the planet.

After Harry cums, he tells me he loves me. It's late in Montreal. I hang up and lie in bed, feeling far away from everyone I've ever known. My jaw throbs. I sit up and look out the window at the empty Sky Business Center, the stars quietly eating themselves.

I have this fear that there's somehow a tape of me walking in a straight line, saying the alphabet backwards and then zipping through an IQ test before looking into the camera and saying, *Actually, yes.* As if I blacked out being lucid. But my memory is a rabbit warren, winding and dark, gaps between the images. A ripped tissue toilet seat cover in the bathroom of the karaoke joint. Blank. Swaying in the parking lot, nauseated from someone's cigarette, feeling stupid and ashamed because I knew I was drunker than everyone else. Blank. Saying yes to a party. Blank. Recognizing, but not understanding, that the Uber had pulled up to his house instead. Blank. My head lolling, my body half on the bed and half off. I don't know if he could tell I woke up but I don't think so, because the clearest image in my mind is his expression, which was disgust.

My phone buzzes. Ewan writes, "wyd?"

I breathe in six, breathe out six, write back, "nothing."

Typing dots appear and evaporate. I get out of bed and turn the shower on, shave my other leg, my senses heightened, my jaw clenched, waiting for the phone to buzz. As I'm tenderly patting a fifth layer of concealer onto my fresh inky bruise, it does. When I smile, my lip bleeds.

"nothing," he says. "wanna come over?"

Six counts in. Six counts out. "sure."

In summer the air would be clean and bright at the horizon as I round onto the 101. The street sweeping truck would be wiping away all the gutter trash, so dawn breaks on fresh concrete. It's winter, though, and as I circle the block looking for parking, I feel deeply, suddenly, convinced the sun will never rise. It could be 3am or 8pm. I could be anyone.

I park in a red zone, too close to the corner but not explicitly unsafe. An excuse to leave early. I'll be in control, home before Harry's even awake.

I try to whistle while I walk, but it's immediately lost, the wind like a mouth on mine. The cold air brings the heat of my injury into startling clarity, the pain sharp and clean.

Ewan's apartment is in one of the East Hollywood '20s buildings that straddle the line between historical treasure and coding violation, with their original crown molding and shitty pipes.

"i'm here," I message him. I have heartburn. I need to eat less spaghetti.

The status flickers from delivered to read.

And the inner door opens, the light flicking on above me, and then the outer door. And there he is. A face and a name, backlit by a long hallway where all the doors are closed.

"What's up," says Ewan, with a watery grin.

"I was just getting some work done," I say, as I follow him down the hall. I can hear animated talking from behind a door, a fight or a TV show, and then it's gone, and he's opening a door and I'm walking into a small square of studio that reeks of ammonia and nicotine. I automatically put my hand over my mouth and then put it down again, embarrassed.

"Some girls have Anthropologie houses, and I get so nervous before they come over," Ewan says. "But I knew you weren't like that. How do we know each other?" He hands me a can of Budweiser and we sit on opposite sides of the sofa.

"Internet, I guess," I say. I crack my beer and he puts on music. I realize I haven't said anything about my face. "Bike," I say.

"What?" I point to my face. He seems to notice it for the first time. "Oh." He has this way of looking at me, his expressions coming into clarity gradually, like a film negative in a chemical bath. I can't tell what he's thinking, how he expects things to go, and it occurs to me that maybe he has no agenda. Or maybe he does, one as pointed and insidious as mine. Except now that I'm here, I can't remember my lines. Everything feels like a bad table read, like I've forgotten which part I'm supposed to be playing. If this were a daytime crime drama, I would be the hardened, wise-cracking detective, probably, because I always identify with the detective. Or I'd be the femme fatale, with her ulterior motives. What would that make Ewan?

We sip our beers. He bounces his knee, jiggling with whatever song is playing. There are long silences, so when we do talk, it sticks to everything. He didn't do anything today, he says, and I say I didn't either. I grasp for something that will give me leverage, something to stand on.

"I have a boyfriend," I say.

"Okay," says Ewan.

"He's in Canada."

"For how long?"

"I dunno. I mean it's clerical. He was supposed to get a lawyer, but he's not getting one, and I don't know." And then I tell him I'm worried Harry left the turtles with me on purpose. I'm worried I'll leave the house and get hit by a car, and they'll die a slow and painful death of neglect. I'm worried because I can't stop them from growing any bigger, and I can't get rid of them, and I can't stop caring but that won't stop them from suffering.

Ewan listens. When I stop, he turns away, twisting to crush a cigarette in a plastic ashtray.

"Sorry," I say.

"I get it," he says. He lights another cigarette, and he tells me a story about a childhood dog. I wait for the part where these universes intersect, but it doesn't happen. The dog lived happily for seventeen years.

Ewan tells me he was a writer on one season of a children's show about a ragtag team of street dogs. I say I worked in television, too, but he cuts me off, explaining my old job back to me. I try to keep up, find the meaning in his anecdotes, the subtext beneath his recitation of the song that the riches-to-rags poodle sang and that still brings in residuals. My brain feels opaque and rubbery, like the white part of a hard-boiled egg. In the crime drama in my mind, there's a bare room, a tape recorder, a cop with a tiny notebook. *Just the facts, ma'am.* My nose is swollen from the shy girl's fist, and the cat piss scent stings.

Once I watched a low-budget mini-doc on YouTube about an experiment where sight was surgically restored to a group of blind patients. Every patient made a full physical recovery, but overwhelmingly, these subjects now found themselves deeply at odds with the world and its irrational spaces. They were baffled by concepts like shape, length, and distance. So distorted was the perspective of some, that seeing an object induced the unpleasant physical sensation of touching their eyes to it. The world was not what the subjects had expected. The vast majority of these patients, the narrator explained in slow, gravelly tones, committed suicide. The experiment failed. What was the experiment trying to achieve, I had wondered, but the narrator never said.

Ewan spreads his knees so one touches mine. He wants to know if I want to watch a movie.

The whole world is a machine, it seems, this universe of iron and expansion. Arranging my jaw muscles to casually ask where the bathroom is feels excruciating, my enunciation off, the conversational black hole opening up again and threatening to suck me into it as I cross the room in front of him.

The bathroom has stucco walls, pubes on the toilet seat and a damp towel hanging on the back of the door. I notice his toothbrush looks wet, and I wonder if he brushed his teeth for me. I notice the hives on my neck are back.

I pee and wipe and feel awful about what I'd said about the turtles, like I had betrayed them. I'm the problem— I control their survival. I can't control anything. Maybe that's how God feels. An orb seeing foregone conclusions in all directions. I am looking down the cylinder of the past, seeing nothing.

Ewan's sink has concentric ruddy stains on the bottom and soap scum caked into the grout. I twist the faucet to find an obliterating heat. The music edges into the room from outside, where Ewan is smoking a cigarette. I plug the sink with a hardened rubber stopper, wet my hands and rub them over my eyes, my cheeks, my lip when it splits again and I start bleeding into the sink bowl.

In another world, I am being held very tenderly. In another one, I am walking back into the living room and silently straddling Ewan. Then jabbing him in the eyes. He fights back but I have the advantage, as smooth as a wave and then a crash and then foamy oblivion. In a different universe, I am walking back to the car, beautiful and alone, watching the lights at the gas station fracture over the quivering leaves of native trees.

I put my lip under the faucet, then my whole face, water in my eyes and ears and mouth, choking on it. It splashes and then pools. I feel it rising. A blank screen and a lapse in memory and a cavernous cosmic void. In another world I'm carrying the little tank into a garden. My childhood sliders basking, huge and lazy in the winter sun. They make it to the water, to the far shore. They survive, even if that means they ravage everything they touch. I expand—a star, a bright collapse in a black night.

3:40PM

Sam Pink

And then, like it always does, the conversation turns to horrific injury and tragedy.

It's just me—rotating/stocking the beer cooler—and a couple contractors at the bar.

One guy has the Fighting Irish logo tattooed on his neck and the other guy had metallic teeth.

Fighting Irish is talking about how if ever anything gets lodged in your chest, you know, don't take it out.

He has his hands up to his chest, as if knifed.

"When you take it out, that's when you die," he says. He mentions a celebrity who'd been stung by a stingray and how, had he gone to surgery, they could've saved him. But they pulled it out right there. "If you pull the thing out, you know, you die," he says, Rumpleminze sipper paused at lips, other hand up as disclaimer.. "As long as that thing is in there, your heart can still work around it. It might be at 50%, but it'll work."

"Yhup," says the other guy. "Y'all member when guardrails wun curved? When the ins wun curved?"

He tells us about a friend he had, who fell asleep at the wheel, in the days before the ends of guardrails were curved, and it ran through the front of his car and into his chest.

The police had to call his mother to the scene, because he was alive as long as the guardrail was in him.

I break down a box, staring.

Fighting Irish says, "Yeah like I said, as long as the thing is in there, your kind of okay. I mean you'll still be alive. The heart works around it. The heart can operate at 50%. Shit, hospitals, the fuggin world, are filled with people whose hearts work 50% and they're alive."

On TV, a man catches a football in spectacular fashion.

Some women in matching uniforms dance for him.

Things exploded.

I think about my heart and what percentage it operates at.

Determining it's either ten percent or one hundred and ten percent.

I visualize it speared, but then immediately see a ring on the end of that, ready to be pulled when it's time to blow everything to hell.

And it all explodes back to the present.

Where I'm staring at a commercial for a sitcom.

"Tab me out when ya get a chance, man," says Fighting Irish.

"Sure thing," I say.

RADIO CURE

Chris Molnar

We were driving from Las Vegas to Los Angeles, as we'd do whenever we could while Kaye lived with me there, in the heat of the summer when you couldn't go outside anywhere within two hundred miles beside the top of Mt. Charleston (all dry bone woods and cabins, dull and beautiful). Leaving as early as we could rouse ourselves, 4 or 5 in the morning to make the most of the weekend, to beat the traffic, or at least head some of it off, hurtling out of the insular, receding lights of Vegas, so small and no longer signifying anything at that hour of the night, blinking to each other and then off, one after the other, the tall beam of the Luxor last as the pale sun rises beyond the mountains. In the desert installations blinked in the still dark, military bases and power plants and radar, still and silent in the day, hardly discernable against the rocks and debris, but powerful and mysterious at night. Jet fighters overhead, on lonely curious missions. We would bring bags of cocaine to keep ourselves awake on the car ride, powering up from sleep into the beyond.

Once I hit one hundred I put the car in neutral and she ripped out the keys. The car made a horrible groaning sound and the smell of oil crept in. With one fluid movement she dipped into the bag of coke and lifted the key up to my nose. I took a long sniff, licked the key, and shoved it back in the ignition. The car started, going sixty down the freeway, then up a dune. I remember it was difficult to seem serious unless I was funny too, as if I had to seem like I was hiding something to be sincere. She cared because I scared her, and she was scared because she cared, and both things were tied together by the joke. I knew the blow hadn't quite kicked in because I would doze for a few seconds before waking up with the neon lights of gas stations filling my vision. I could hear her heartbeat under the blast of the AC; the radio was falling out of reach; only her irregular breathing and the sonorous foreign tongue between stations, spoken steadily like a great ancient machine, all curving metal and webbed grating, gears and wires, pedals and wheels.

"Have you fucked anyone else?" I asked.

"Did you know that no brake marks mean suicide?" she remarked, gazing off at some tire tread scattered on the side of the road. I turned the wheel quickly as if in commentary, flipping on the CD player as the dawn crept up behind us. The clicks and random noise beginning D'Angelo's *Voodoo*.

"Business school people. The consultant types. I'd understand."

She shook her head, looked me in the eye, and put a hand on my crotch. I inhaled, stared dully out at the road then mumbled half to myself "Barstow, thirty-five miles... hobo capital..." Blinking, I made myself alert and reached over to touch her in response; her hand immediately slackened and she began to pant slightly.

"Sure you didn't fuck anyone else?" I asked again.

Kaye opened her eyes (grey-green, I had never noticed before) and looked at me with a droll, piercing look, shaking her head. As I slackened my hand she looked behind us into the rising pink-white.

"Is someone following us?"

I took out the key again on the downhill, the horrible neutral noise and sweet-sick smell returning. A Nevada State Police car cruised by going far over a hundred, then into the distance. Kaye dipped into the bag again for me and held it up to my nose.

"Maniac cop," I said, then, "thanks."

"Keep going," she said, grabbing my wrist. I undid her zip.

I remembered biking slowly on acid around Las Vegas while she was away, in the encroaching still hotness of late spring, thinking about how I've got to be good, we only have each other, long echoing chambers of experience, straight and drug-induced, surrounding two naked, credulous people at the core, moist and bright and sort of Asian and probably damaged somehow. Thinking about how "distance has no way of making love understandable". About her loneliness, and mine, and how loneliness can override commitment, about Mona, the open mic girl who looked like Lauryn Hill, who I could laugh easy with, who could keep up with me but never had a harsh word. And then some tourists threw an In-N-Out cup full of lemonade at me and I crashed my bike.

In the car I could feel Kaye reach some agreement with her body, the gathering electricity as she pulled her thighs together and then released. We sat next to each other as she closed her eyes in the dawning blue.

LIVESTREAM

Elle Nash

I made plans to drive to my parents' house in Bend, Oregon, a dirty white clapboard on the corner of a street with no name and miles of wired fence. I drive through Nebraska, I drive through Colorado, I drive through Wyoming and Montana. Between Denver and Bozeman there is nothing, a big nothing. The sky is filament above me.

Bozeman is my stop for the night. Main Street is a slip off the highway and a slip back on and in any other moment the town would be gone in an instant. I get out at a rest stop and look at the sky, the impossible sky, which hangs higher than it seems in other places, as if the glass that makes the atmosphere keeps the clouds further away from the ground. Everything around tinged pale yellow from the setting sun. A man at the rest stop takes a second glance and I wipe soured milk from the sides of my mouth, dust crumbs from my abdomen. I think of myself as a single mother already, conscious of my youth, my round belly accentuating the youth of my soft cheeks. I am only slightly showing. In my car, remnants of the trip: crusted coffee cups, food trash, a bottle of vitamins on the seat, a duffel bag with the insides spilling out.

In the parking lot of an Australian steakhouse franchise, I turn off the car and the heat wraps around me like sheet plastic. Other cars pull in, people amble towards the entrance. The hostess is my age, shoulder length brown hair, wide hips, smooth skin. She taps her pen against a clipboard as she asks if anyone else will be joining me. I say no. She keeps tapping and looks down at a map of the restaurant. My lips are chapped; I bring my hand to my mouth again. I imagine the feel of her lips parting as the tips of my fingers graze against dried lip-skin. Some part of me wants to ask her for a job application. The foyer is air-conditioned and I rub my shoulders pink.

She sits me at a booth and gives me a large, laminated menu. I watch as the lint on the back of her black trousers sashays away. I fantasize about what it would be like to stay in Bozeman, to live her life. I wonder if it is better or different than mine, if she is dating anyone. If her parents are nice. If she thinks about the future.

Of course she does all of these things. I take a sip of ice water, my hand wet with condensation, and think about who I have left behind: a man I thought I loved. I wear a ring on my finger, but we haven't married. I am supposed to be planning a wedding. I am supposed to be in love. I am supposed to stop lying about how I pay the bills. Instead I leave the apartment in the middle of the night, I turn my phone on airplane mode just to disappear off the grid for a few hours. I wake up in the bed of an ex who burns me mixed CDs before placing a white envelope into my purse. In bed, the ex rubs my belly, not knowing who resides beneath.

I trace my hands over the sweaty plastic of the menu, touching perfect beef, a fluffed mashed potato, a wedge of moist cheesecake. Slats of light glare across my table, shift, and then disappear. A waitress walks away from the window directly in front of me, the chain waving from touch. The outline of an industrial park is a burned shadow in the blinds.

My future now stands before me like a city of tall buildings. Everything is already built. There is no changing the location of skyscrapers. I can see them in the distance. One building is the birth process, the pain and fear of the unknown; one building is a career path; one building is a job with no upward mobility; one building is retirement and savings; one is my relationship with _____.

One building is a mortgage, yet another terrifying building is the health of my aging parents, the decreasing lucidity of my mother. The tallest building is the child itself, as it will become the singular responsibility that will define my life.

I order perfect beef with a forty-four ounce caramel-colored diet soda and a baked potato with butter, sour cream, bacon. I drink down the complimentary glass of water. I stare at my cell phone, navigate to one social media site after another, post updates about scheduling a livestream. The waitress brings my meal and smiles at me with lipstick on her teeth and I smile back wishing I could be her friend, wishing I could rent a hotel room here and never leave.

I could do whatever I wanted, but I don't.

I sit my cell phone up against the frosted glass of soda, camera pointed on my meal, the little red light on the screen flashing, numbers counting up to one minute, then one minute and a half, then two minutes, then two and a half.

Meal is such a disgusting word to describe the act of eating.

I eat cubes of steak, the potato next, then broccoli, washed down with another glass of water, pause the video, drink the diet soda, and leave cash on the table.

The restroom door is heavy and the lacquer is tacky against my hands, fluorescent light reflected on the beige tiles inside, a geometric row of stalls. The lights flicker like a fly beating its wings and it is as though I can see and I cannot see at the same time. Like a dream. I lock the door behind me in the stall, having to lift and place the door shut. I place my cell phone on the stainless steel receptacle for sanitary napkins and tampons and un-pause the livestream. I look at the camera without speaking, smile and remember the porn star I watched the night before at a motel in Colorado Springs, how she got choke-fucked in the face by some nameless, disposable pair of legs with a dick attached, her mascara smeared into the creases of her eyes, and every time she vomited (did she have a gag reflect, still, after all of that?), the useless pair of legs would produce an arm that swept up all of the spit and vomit and slapped it onto her face. Her pigtails torn and pulled, she sat there, a moment of hesitation before placing her fake nail to her mouth, California-bright teeth glaring as her lips split into a smile. I smile for the camera this way, push fingers down my throat, reach for the reflex.

The sound of a cartoon coin being collected rings from the phone. I am getting tipped. Every tip nets fifty cents to a couple of dollars. I have to push harder and harder into my throat, the reflex dying from overuse, leaving teeth marks on my knuckles, the two fingers flailing harder inside the spitty cave of my throat.

I look from the toilet to the phone and bloodshot eyes meet me, my hand fisting my mouth, chats floating in and out of existence. More tips ring. Everything kicks and I push harder, and it kicks, empty, like a hiccup, and I push harder, my abdomen squeezing, and I wonder about the fetus inside, if it feels hugged and warm, and then everything comes up in hard, square chunks: the broccoli, raw and confetti like, the potatoes in solid lumps, sticking to everything. My eyes sparkle and blink. More anonymous tips. More tips. More tips. I think of _____.

The single ply toilet paper crumbs from my fists like sunburn skin. I turn off the livestream, and stand up to wash my hands. When I open the bathroom door, the hostess is standing at the sink, but seems surprised, as if she hadn't known I was there. I imagine her waiting for me, leaning against the wall, listening to the retching sounds and cartoon coin drops pinging every few seconds. She dries her hands and leaves the bathroom without making eye contact. I walk to my car and check my account and tally the tips, but it is not enough to score a room for the night. Back on the road a storm threatens to burst and I find a truck stop somewhere between Bozeman and Idaho Springs. I park the car on the dark side of the gas station, the clouds flickering above, thunder a distant gurgle. I press my hands into my stomach, the bulb of growth inside me, and feel as empty as the sky.

THE ROMAN SOLDIER

B.R. Yeager

We did it as a joke. Renting the Westfield Econo Lodge jacuzzi room. A joke, but not really. I'd mentioned it to Brian maybe a month earlier, coming back to his place from a bowl ride. "I'm gonna rent a jacuzzi room for my birthday."

He laughed. "What?"

"We can like drink and smoke in there. No one will bother us. It'll be funny. It's a jacuzzi room."

He laughed again. "Okay dude."

I told Efrim later that week, over at his dad's place. I pushed open his door and he looked up from his computer, cracked lips and sink hole eyes. He hadn't slept in days, obliterating his father's liquor cabinet and recording songs about the Jordanian Civil War.

"I'm renting a jacuzzi room for my birthday."

His eyes went live. He smiled the way a mask smiles. "A jacuzzi room?"

"Yeah, at the Westfield Econo Lodge."

He stomped out his cigarette on the hardwood and giggled, making a goblin face. "That's so fucking stupid."

Seth called the day of, while me and Efrim were coming out of Liquors 44. "What are you jerks up to?"

"I'm with Efrim," I said. "It's my birthday."

"That's delightful. Happy birthday. You need any buttsex?" Our codeword for weed ("Soapy buttsex" if it was good shit). Because cops are less likely to follow you into the woods if they overhear you talking about "getting into some sketchy buttsex," but obviously that's a lie. It was stupid. It was funny.

"Yeah, absolutely. I'm renting a jacuzzi room. We've got some liquor."

"You're renting a jacuzzi room?"

"At the Westfield Econo Lodge. You want in?"

Silence, then laughter. "Okay, sure. I'm in. Pick me up at my place."

* * *

Everything I'd ever done was for someone else's enjoyment. In third grade I stuffed my fingers down my throat, forcing a stream of puke (leftover hot and sour soup from Chinese takeout) onto the lunch table. The cafeteria came to life with disgust and awe. When I was twelve I told the drama club I jacked off ten times a day (a lie—I hadn't once successfully masturbated, still unsure of the mechanics, of the necessary vigor to let the white out). A gift—something for them to joke about. Two years later I'd tell my closest circle about the watermelon I hollowed out and fucked (another fabrication—I still didn't understand masturbation, and wouldn't until after high school). They gleefully tormented me for years.

This was my purpose. I was sure of it. People won't keep you close out of love. But destroying yourself, letting others destroy you—it keeps them from hating you completely.

* * *

The sign evoked a hospital, or a barbershop—words and bars in red and white. Centuries ago hospitals and barbershop were the same thing, more or less—you'd go to the barber for shaves and cuts, but also bloodletting and amputation. That's why the poles look like candy canes.

The structure below was beige stucco and deep green roofing. Sickly trees clawing out from mulch. It sat between the I-90 off ramp and a Wendy's, overlooking Westfield—a gasping town, a murdered town, with streets and avenues full of feral dogs and monsters dressed in people's skin. An apocalypse happened there, was still happening, and no one quite knew what to do. So they climbed the tallest hill they could find and built an Econo Lodge on top. A retreat, an oasis you could afford.

We tore into the parking lot, sliding into a spot between a Humvee and a Pontiac station wagon. Efrim wanted to come in with me to register. He hated the idea of me doing anything without him. I told Seth to stay in the car.

"Why?"

"It's sketchy if it's three people."

"How is three sketchier than two?"

"If they see three guys renting a one-bed jacuzzi room, they're gonna think it's sketchy."

"Anyone who rents a jacuzzi room at the fucking Westfield Econo Lodge is going to look sketchy."

"Just stay in the car. We'll be right back."

A grey weed miasma poured from the car, quickly diluting in the hot garbage air, and we headed in. The reception reeked of bleach, stabbing up my nose and scraping at my throat. The woman at the desk looked like Peter Cook but prettier. "Can I help you?" A voice that'd been choked. A collapsed voice—one that knew, deeply knew the world was ending, but you still got to pay bills. You still have to show up. We weren't old enough to understand, to recognize how much we had in common with this woman. We still thought our lack of franchise was temporary, that our best days were still in our futures. That one day, if we played our cards right, every day would be like this one.

"Yeah, do you have any jacuzzi rooms?" I held in my laughter, but Efrim giggled at my side, gently bucking forward and back.

The woman's face stayed neutral. "Let me look." Dried apricot hands tapped across the keyboard. "Do you want the square jacuzzi or the heart-shaped one?"

Efrim cackled. "Oh, you gotta get the heart shaped one."

"Yeah, I'll take the heart shaped." She copied my ID and took my cash.

* * *

It was exactly what you'd expect: creamy, mold-speckled wallpaper peeling where the walls and ceiling met; a charcoal carpet with grey and wine accents. A bed and two chairs. And wedged into the corner, set before two streaked wall-length mirrors: a concave, dog-dick-red heart, encased in concrete and tile. Its bottom coated in chalky grey stains.

"Whooaaa," Seth said. "This is pretty, pretty, pretty grimy."

"No." Efrim ran his hands over the tub's lip. "It's perfect." He twisted the jacuzzi knobs and steaming grey water thundered out.

I flipped on the bedside lamp—the shade runny with weird amber resin—and punched the A/C down to 60°. The unit shuddered and gasped. I filled the bathroom sink with ice and stuck the Smirnoff and Bloody Mary mix in. The OJ wouldn't fit, so I took off the top of the toilet tank, poured down some ice and lay the bottle on top.

* * *

It's easy to get drunk fast if you want it to be. Orange juice neutralizes the choke of vodka, so you can down at least three Solo cups of the stuff in under 5 min, you won't gag, it won't twist your stomach. That's how clean it tastes. You can drink and drink and it'll only taste better the more you drink. Still young in our abuse, years before our guts would be ravaged by ulcer and abscess. I don't miss those days (I can't, it's impossible), but I know Efrim does.

* * *

Three screwdrivers and two bowls and the steaming grey water rose to the tub's lip. I shut off the faucet and got the bottles from the bathroom, placing them atop the jacuzzi's tiled edge. We stripped. Efrim's wire body practically hairless, all sallow skin, tight starved muscles clinging to bone. Seth wrapped his waist with a towel before disrobing. We turned on the jets and slipped in.

Efrim and I sunk into each of the heart's butt cheeks, while Seth sat at the point. Cramped, but as long as we clung to our corners we wouldn't touch. Any touching would need to be deliberate and ironic. "It isn't gay if people are watching" I'd told Efrim once, wobbling drunk at some dance night (no, I know the precise one), before sucking on his disgusting tobacco-resined lips. Everyone around us laughed.

I poured another round. The heat climbed into my skin, mixing with the liquor, strengthening its power. Water pounded at my vertebrae, punching gently at my discs. I touched myself beneath the murk of the jets, where no one could see.

*   *   *

"Shit I'm fucked up." I pointed to Seth. "Is tonight gonna be a bad night?"

Seth looked down and away.

I nudged Efrim's elbow. "Seth and I get fucking *bad* when we drink together."

"We don't need to talk about that," Seth said.

"Like two years back? We got this bum to buy us growlers. Fucking plowed through them shits like nothing, so quick we didn't even know we were wasted until we stood up. Like *whoooaaaa.* We go outside, smoke some butts, and end up tossing half his dad's firewood into the road."

"Hold on." Seth said. "It was like five pieces of wood."

"Like 15. At least 15. Like 20 pieces. Then we spend the whole night waiting to see if cars will run them over." I laughed. The only one laughing.

"Nothing happened though. I knew nothing was gonna happen."

"Or how 'bout that night at Calamari's? So they used to have this bartender, and he never carded us. So one night we go in there and pound three Long Island Iced Teas. Like one after another. I give this guy a look and we head down to the bathroom, like this shitty basement bathroom, and we do a little coke. Next thing we know, we're *fucking that place up*. I'm talking smashing the goddamn mirror, I'm puking in the air dryers, just out of fucking control. It was like fucking Fallujah."

"Come on man."

I slapped Seth on his shoulder. "This guy's a fucking monster when he drinks. At least when he drinks with me."

"Stop."

"What? These are classics. It's fun. This is fun."

Efrim frowned, eyes away from us. Looking at himself through the fog in the mirrors. Not disgusted. He didn't care about strangers' tires popping over splintered wood, or the poor barback who'd have to clean up me and Seth's wrath. He didn't care about those things. He was only jealous. He always was jealous, of any world existing without him. He still is, and will always be.

* * *

8 months back at Seth's 21st birthday, he dropped acid and sliced a cigarette out of his girlfriend's mouth with a katana. Weeks ago he saved an elderly woman who'd collapsed face-first in the Stop & Shop parking lot. Her glasses snapped apart, wire frames sticking in her retina. I didn't tell those stories. Those were hero stories, and I didn't care if Efrim knew them.

* * *

We drank another round, smoked another bowl, ripped around three more butts, just ashing over the side onto the carpet. Seth's head lolled, nodding forward before snapping back. "I feel like I'm gonna pass out." He stood up, wobbly, lifting one leg over the side of the red heart and tile, dropping his foot down on the blackened carpet. Glistening thick thighs, belly and ass. He pulled a towel from the floor and wrapped himself quick.

I swigged from my cup. My head swam and throat ached, cracked. "Yeah, not a bad idea." I stood up.

"You fucking *pussy*." Efrim put on a faggy lisp, like he always did when we were drunk and around other people. "Come back here and stop being *such a fucking pussy*." He grabbed my wrist and gave it a yank.

My feet skidded, my knees buckled, but they didn't fall out. "I'm gonna crack my fucking head." I pulled away, my wrist slipping from his fingers, nearly toppling backward over the rim.

Efrim squinted, cutting his mouth into a frown. He'd given me the same look the last time we'd done mushrooms, when he grabbed a kitchen knife and jokingly waved it at me, before winking and putting it back in the drawer. He raised his fists and leaned forward.

"Don't." I put my hands up in front of me.

He giggled through the creased frown and pushed forward, swinging a long stringy arm, slapping me just between my crotch and belly.

"No, fucking stop. Knock it off." But this was what drew us to each other's orbits. The constant push and pull. Always competing for the room. Gobbling up each other's air, just sucking it out of every space we occupied.

"Maybe we should be a little more quiet?" Seth said.

Efrim turned and splashed water toward him and the bed. "Sweetie, the only people here are lawyers and their whores. It's fine."

I stepped down onto the carpet (soaked and slimy, like something alive), a miasma churning against my skin, space pulsing against my eyes (the vodka in my blood circulating through me, top to bottom, limb to limb, over and over). I grabbed a washcloth from the floor and tied it around my balls and outer thigh, so only the side of my sack was visible. I asked Seth (sprawled across the bed, a round leg peeking through his bath towel, like a gutter Frazetta cheesecake piece) if he wanted another drink.

He grimaced, but then: "Yeah, sure. A Bloody Mary. I didn't eat today."

I grabbed the bottles, filling half his Solo cup with vodka and the other half with Bloody Mary mix. I dug into a grocery bag and tossed him a bag of potato chips. Then I grabbed the disposable camera. Dew beads clung to it, like it'd been sweating.

Seth ignored the drink and tore open the chips, scooping fistfuls into his mouth. I lifted the camera to my face, framing his sprawled wet body in a tiny black box—a tiny diorama inside the viewfinder. He stopped eating. "What are you doing?"

"Documenting our *love*," I said, misquoting a movie I otherwise couldn't remember. I wound the advance. Click. Flash. Captured.

"Don't let him have all the fun." Efrim rose from the tub, still in that raging queen affect. He lifted his leg, standing his foot on the jacuzzi's lip, like Teddy Roosevelt perched on a bear carcass. The heat dragged his ball sack toward his knee. An old man's sack. I turned the camera toward him. Click click click. He lifted his palm to just beneath his chin and blew a kiss. Through the black box of the viewfinder, he looked doused in blood.

* * *

Brian and Roy swang by. I answered the door in my washcloth loin cloth and Brian's face melted with equal parts inspiration and disgust. He looked past me, over our wreckage. "Jesus Christ." Roy just stared down at his shoes, clenching and unclenching his jaw.

Efrim flung a thin knobby finger at Brian. "Why don't you get more comfortable." He pushed past me, rushing him, grasping onto his belt.

"No. No no no." Brian pushed back at Efrim's hands, laughing but some real panic there too.

I went for Roy, hands outstretched toward his crotch. He grimaced, almost smiling, but mostly grit teeth, shaking his head. "If you touch me I'm gonna fucking belt you."

Efrim made a few more lazy gropes at Brian before slapping his ass, hard and loud—a real clap. He teetered backward in the heat, face turned slick and lazy, sloshing toward mine, rapist eyes, a gaping rapist grin. He lumbered into me, pushing his belly into mine, gyrating sweaty and slick. I pressed further into him, my belly slipping off and around his starved concave pelvis. "Oh here's the real man," he said. He started humping. A joke. Blood rushed to my shaft. My balls slipped out from the washcloth and slapped the inside of his thigh. A joke.

"Jesus Christ." Brian laughed and clapped, red-faced, pushing past us, looking away and then looking back. "You should just give him the Roman Soldier and get it over with."

Efrim stopped and squeezed my shoulders (those enormous neanderthal hands), like he could yank my flesh right off the muscle. His mouth became a circle, an O, a perfect round void punched through his face. His eyes went wild like when I first told him about the jacuzzi room. "Dude."

I didn't say anything.

"Dude," he repeated. "We have to."

"I don't know man."

"We have to. Don't be a bitch."

"Let me piss first." I slipped out of Efrim's hands and into the bathroom. My piss sputtered toxic orange into the pristine pool. So dehydrated. Through the walls, I could hear them all talking, then laughing. Someone—Efrim—hushing them. Then bad stage whispers. Laughing again. I flushed and came back out and they all stopped and stared at me, smiling.

* * *

We found it online. No pics, just a .txt file. This collection of sex positions. At least half were fake, like ones no one could've possibly done. Like the Disrespectful Winston—you fist a girl (or a guy, I guess) in the ass, get a fistful of shit and rub it in her face, like *Look what you did. You should be ashamed of yourself.* Or the Teleporter: you bang a girl (or a guy, I guess) doggystyle, facing a window, and you swap out with a different guy with the same sized dick. Then you creep outside, go around to the window and wave while the other guy keeps plowing her. Probably no one's ever done that either.

But Efrim's favorite was simple and entirely plausible. When he first read it off to me, the image snapped together in my head like one of those cheap 3D animations. Click. I cackled. Efrim cackled with me. We told it to our other friends, who cackled too. Simple and perfect, like an orchid, or a scalpel. Like all the best jokes.

* * *

I laid down on the floor, the whole carpet saturated, soaked and slimy and cold. Brian wound the disposable camera's advance. Click click click.

Roy leaned over me. "You sure you want to do this dude?"

I sat up. "Can I get another swig?"

Efrim handed me the vodka. Even though it was almost gone, the bottle felt heavier now than when I had bought it. I took my swig. I could barely even taste the burn at that point. I handed it back. "Alright," he said. Face scrunched, shaking giddy. "You ready?"

"Yeah, sure. I guess."

"You heard'em." He stood over my face. A strange inverted valley between his legs. A sacred mountain. All my futures. He unbuckled his knees and began descending.

"Jesus Christ," Brian said. "Holy shit."

Efrim lifted and held his cock. His hips descended lower, lower, closer, closer, until it almost smothered the light. I closed my eyes.

Warmth. Insane warmth. One sac over one eye, and then the other. Soft loose flesh like a grandmother's throat. A weird reek—of shit and sweat, but also beyond those scents. But it was the warmth, this fleshy sticky fucking warmth on my face. Warmth like heaven. A pink pig draped over my face.

"Holy shit," Seth said.

Then down, draped across my nose. A pungent tube. Hot as a stroke. A thimble's worth of sticky fluid dribbled from its end, down my septum.

It was done. A ball over each eye. His cock down my nose. I became the Roman Soldier.

The shutter clicked. The room screamed and laughed. The flesh jiggled on my face, but didn't let up. I could hear Efrim hushing everyone. He whispered. "So … lift … hold … I'll …"

"What's going on?" I said. His crotch reek slipped into my mouth, sour like mold.

"Nothing," Efrim said. "Just a second." More whispering. "Don't let … the rest …"

"Yo I think I'm done here."

"Okay, okay." The flesh lifted off my face. I opened my eyes, black becoming brown becoming the room, the mold-speckled ceiling. Efrim stared down, bloody eyes, teeth locked in gaping crescent. "Happy birthday." He raised the Smirnoff bottle above his head and brought it down.

Crack.

The world goes hot. Hot and wet. *Crack.* The world becomes slick and hot and gaping. *Crack.* I throw my limbs up in front of me. I try to scream but a thick round knee drops onto my throat. *Crack.* The world becomes two sets of hands holding me down. *Crack.* The world is glass against skin and hair, becoming glass against bone. *Crack.* The world is my nose plunging down into my face. My teeth snapping apart against the thick glass. *Crack.* Booted feet stomping on my ribs and crotch. The world is grunts and laughter. *Crack.* The world is caved-in ribs and burst testicles. *Crack.* My skull breaks before the glass does. When the bottle finally falls to splinters, Efrim yanks the phone off the nightstand and pounds my face until it's no longer a face, until it's no longer anything. They stand there, heaving, inhaling the mist, the reek of mold and piss and shit and brains, they huddle over my body, they hug and they laugh.

* * *

It's something they'll always remember. Something for when they're old, a reminder of what it's like to be young. Brian and Roy finally strip, they hold their dicks and piss on my body, into the broken hole that used to be my face. They'll pose with my body, snapping pictures, knowing they'll never be developed, that the camera will be burned in the bedside trash can. They'll watch the sunrise from the balcony, streaked with blood, smoking cigarettes and the last of Seth's buttsex, telling each other secrets they'd never shared with anyone and never will again, laughing and crying, holding each other, kissing each other's foreheads and cheeks with dry, ripped up lips. Saying how much they love each other. They will pull my body onto the bed, fill the sheets with toilet paper and towels and set it alight. They'll leave, loading into Roy's car and setting off onto the highway, dropping everyone at their respective homes. They will sleep the rest of the day, wrapped in cotton cocoons while the A/C flushes out the summer fever. Or maybe they won't sleep at all, shivering, replaying the night over and over, sometimes giggling, sometimes completely still. None of them will ever speak my name again.

BENZAITEN

Aristilde Kirby

<u>A</u>.

I breathed calmly to myself, ran through all the places I could be, including here. I looked at her eyepatch, leather, bandaged with a fur of some sort on the interior. I never heard about how she lost what no longer lies beneath. No one knew. People projected, however, whatever they wanted into the space of its absence. Whatever for a second seemed to make sense. Or not. Each wisp of hearsay came & went like the wind till it was unnoticed. I noticed Laharla's face glow in the jump cuts of the sun, then more & more orange.

An explosion rocked the car's trajectory, favoring more my side. We were all shaken a bit just the same. Laharla snapped to look out the back window.

"Princess. The bastards are back."

I could hear espadrilles bear down on the roof of the car.

Flashes of light erupted in the distance. No one was driving. What else did I have to lose except the life I hadn't made for myself yet?

<u>B.</u>

"So this is what'll happen. We're going to do one a variation of one of the Lispector Tests first: the Agua Viva Faucet Exam. Measuring your endurance & dexterity," Laharla said, closing the window.

She continued: "I'll whisper you some details about my past life, from different eras…"
The AC hummed below in the distance.

"…& you'll exact it in prose with the parameters in mind, turning on a dime."
Our cups of tea were no longer giving off steam.

"When you're done, I'll look it over, & we'll head to the next section."

"…Give me that spring Hudson from a faucet.
Run on until I tell you to stop, & we'll switch gears. "

I could feel the demon princess breathe in my ear.

I gave a gulp & got started:

"Princess Laharla (formerly known as Aristilde Kirby, née Andrew Kirby) was a transgender artist. Born in the Bronx, New York on April 11, 1991 at Bronx Lebanon Hospital. She had a rough start, fighting with other boys, getting in trouble for drawing penises & the word sex in dictionaries. She first liked a girl named Sylvia, with green eyes, dirty blonde hair.

He got her start as a writer writing fan-fiction related to Megaman & Final Fantasy in 2nd grade.

She was an avid Pokémon player, going so far as to organize a Game Boy tournament played in lunch period, advertised by posters he made in art class.

She stole money from his mother to buy Pokémon cards & was placed on punishment the entire summer in 3rd grade.

She died, wracked with guilt, boiling in long steeping misery stemming from a life of myriad hardships, in a suicide where she ran her mechanically ailing white Ford Focus she paid $2000 in student loan money for. She ran her Ford Focus, named Monique (Wittig), through the hill barrier on Mount Merino Road, vaulting into & through trees, her car crushed in somersaults on the rocks, her body ejected through the windshield into the Hudson.

Her body was found awash beneath the dock of the lighthouse, covered in seaweed & wounds.

He at least partly reformed, becoming Vice President on the Student Council beneath President Francesca, winning a popular vote after making a sandwich sign, going around the entire school getting signatures & raising money & food for the homeless. This got her put in the school newspaper. Her favorite field trip was to the Bronx Zoo, where she got a tiger mask.

She got circumcised at 6, & when she plucked the stitches from her penis, it seemed to her like the barbwire crowning the building's gated courtyard across the street where her and her friends played basketball & other games. She fell asleep to Biggie Smalls & Eminem every night. She was taken care of after early school days by Ms. Rodriguez, she called him Angel due to her accent. She hung out a lot with friends Catherine & Alberto, her children.

She remembers getting Little Debbie cakes & jug barrel juices for 25 cents at the corner store. He got a bike and not knowing at first, of course not knowing how to ride it, flipped into a pile of trash. She got the hang of it though, eventually. He was envious of Tasia's Barbie Lamborghini that her father gave her, not having a father in his life, having been abandoned with Scarlet Fever after an outing with Mark Wright, the morning when he was fighting with his blonde girlfriend in West Orange, New Jersey.

Aris would walk home after her shifts at the first University of West Georgia dining hall Z6 for two miles in summer heat & winter cold, listening to music, sometimes afraid of her shadow on the ground, thinking someone was creeping up on her, walking down the same road. As was sometimes the case.

Months later, after after-school poetry club activities, Andrew was propositioned by a closeted gay fat band-geek also in the club to suck his dick for 50 dollars, weeping. Aris, at the time, was moved by his suffering & capitulated. Why not. They never spoke again.

Months later, Aris dated a girl named Jeannie. She had green eyes, brown hair. She would always hit on him via Myspace & AIM. He got his mother to drop him off at Atlantic Station, where they would see the movie Across The Universe. They sat in the back, and she fingered Jeannie to the part where they sung Strawberry Fields Forever. She wet the entire seat. A month later, her stepfather called Andrew and told him that Jeannie could not date a black guy. They never spoke again.

Having gotten her bachelor's degree, Aris spent the first two months post-grad being homeless due to an eviction stemming from spiking accumulating late fees in regard to rent. She had lost her job due to a discrepancy with student status at the Registrar's Office during the dining service's transition from the independent company Aramark to being state owned, meaning that due to not being able to take enough credit hours and needing one class to graduate, she could not legally work as a student worker anymore.

She slept in the forest next to the water tower at the place she just graduated to minimize the time walking to school. She packed all her things into a storage unit she paid 50 dollars a month for. She was indebted to the apartment complex. After two Gofundmes, she just accepted her fate.

She was part-time until she graduated, then she was full-time until she left Georgia in May. She didn't tell anyone she was working with she was taking showers in the Geology building bathroom. She didn't tell anyone she was suffering. She would autopilot through shifts. She would walk home every night listening to the song The Self by Richard Spaven in the dead of winter, sleeping on a yoga mat padding a tree root & two blankets. She went to sleep shivering & woke up shivering. She knew what doors she could open on the weekends, where she could be warm, sleep in a classroom before classes for others started, use the internet.

But at least things were happening with writing, finally, right?

Even with an inter & intra-personal meltdown.

After being heavily burnt out with the thought of school, not knowing what else to do, she applied to MFAs from her former Spanish professor's house where she stayed for 3 months.

Having secured an excess of a year's worth of estrogen & spirolactone, she began transitioning 8 years ago, on Valentine's Day.

She bought a mug from the Society6 of Apollonia Sinclair, donning a drawing of a modern reversal of the myth of Leda & The Swan, where the Leda figure takes the Swan by the neck with her hand into her nether region. She drinks tea out of it every day, even right now.

She learned from the Benzaiten of her demon youth that the Avīci Hell of The World is just that, a shadow complement hinged on all of existence as we know it. Hell is a fundamental, seemingly universal experience of religion, a perversion of morality necessary to create shame in people along the most intimate recesses of their lives to enforce conformity to ascribed social standards, to create arbitrary hierarchies in order to give an even slightly plausible, purely fictive logic to essentially meaningless suffering.

A place where suffering is eternal fuel, where blood lubricates the gears of its operations, where every terror imaginable happens to beings whose only evident crime sometimes is simply being born. Where everyone hurts whether they deserve it or not. So long as the human World exists as it does, Hell will for everyone else as well. It is mass-scale extinctions, it is the erosion of the planet, it is the subjugation & genocide of entire peoples & their cultures.

Common sense is what foments & maintains these things, & this metes out private pain of every degree in each gradation. Benzaiten told Aris she was living just another life after death. That there is no escape from the cycle until you put this place in a better shape than it was when you first left.

ASCENDANT

Gina Nutt

The day comes and goes and I'd say it's all the same but I know it isn't. I'm on a sun journey and it's a long one. Weight on my legs wakes me. Perched on the bed edge, Colin kisses my forehead. He nods at the tray bridged over my shins. A plate of warm toaster waffles and enormous strawberries stems off and centers cut out, a star of whipped cream sprayed in the hollows. A mug filled with coffee. A mason jar filled with orange juice.

I slice bites of waffle. Melted butter and syrup spills from the nooks. I unwrap the various shapes filling the empty stretch of sheet where Colin sleeps. A yacht rock album, milky vinyl with blue splatter across it. A necklace with a tiny cat-head silhouette. A bag of gummy worms. The animals rush toward the tearing sound. They leap onto the covers and step all over the crumpled paper. I lean back in bed, picking at my breakfast and starting on a ribbon of Dollar Dog Scratch-eez tickets. Neely noses at the plate. I swoop a finger through the whipped cream and hold my hand out to her. She laps at the white froth melting to my knuckles.

"I've got to get to work," Colin says getting up. He hands me another gift, smiles extra-proud of this one.

"Is it fragile?"

"For the pool."

I turn over the slim bundle, carefully untape the taped places, peel open the white paper with gold flecks to reveal a pair of shiny orange shorts with a white owl on the thigh.

*

Marinating in the water, June informs me this is my "Jesus year." Ever since my Saturn's return stretched several too-long years at the end of my third decade I have wondered why the years must come saddled with big meaning. Stamped like colorful rubber bracelets for any thinkable cause, all that wearable salvation. Birthdays can feel like bad music I listen to when no one else is around. Indulgent, pleasing, and wretched. I like to offset the bad feelings with elaborate unconsummated plans. Trips I don't take. People I mean to call and don't. Parties I don't throw.

Last year I researched airfare and a weekend stay in a mid-state hotel—retro, pink, expensive. The hotel is situated in a region famed for its vintages. The hotel has its own label. I got really into wine. My online searches showed an uptick in queries concerning grapes, tasting notes, and terroir. I went in and out of shops, seeking a dressing gown. I wanted something miraculous—floor-length and sheer, marabou edging sleeves and hem. My longing was too specific. Something to recline in while speaking into a rotary phone.

June asks, "How are your plants?"

"I have several," I gesture up toward the balcony.

"The testers," she says.

"Something's happening, I'm not sure what yet."

"I think mine are duds."

"Anything you keep inside all the time is a dud," I say. "Try them on the balcony."

June keeps talking about the plants we're supposed to be growing, the seeds we're testing for a friend's wedding favors. She talks about dresses and shoes, fitting appointments, message threads displaying inside jokes between people we don't really know.

"Are you excited?"

"For Erin and Luke's wedding?"

"You're birthday."

"It's something," I say and roll off my floatie.

I give up on keeping my hair dry, wing my arms like I'm making a snow angel and sink myself to the pool floor. The sun through the water spreads possibility overhead. Rays like potential, beams of ambition and success. If I look too long, I'll get a headache. I like these days I stay in the complex, save for walking Neely. Phone tucked in the dresser drawer with all my tee shirts, I circle the courtyard path. I repeat, "Doing my best, doing my best" and I'm not sure it's true.

*

Coarse white and gray fur rains into the courtyard. Someone brushes a dog on their balcony. I hear the pins catch in the fur and the owner's apology. The dog understands the sorry even less than the ritual that inspires it. A tuft lands on the plate June and I share. Salami and cheese, peppadews, almonds, olives.

"Do you ever get nervous handing over your ID in a liquor store?" I ask.

She laughs and snaps a cracker off in her teeth.

"Beer with groceries, I'm fine. But I get shaky buying liquor. Not enough to not buy it, but I sweat a little."

"You're too old for that feeling. What's your rising sign?"

"I don't know. But I'm bad at it. What if the person behind the counter decides they don't like anyone's face that day? Then we're all liars."

June's dog, Science, drags a plant up the path. The roots drag on the ground. She drops it between our loungers. The command June delivers, "Leave it," neat and crisp and Science totters off to cause damage elsewhere. I miss saying, "Let's leave it at that" and the leaving actually happening.

*

I shuffle a deck on the balcony. I wait for Colin to arrive with takeout, the sliding door to whisper open and resume my quiet celebration. I'm bad at birthdays. So much expectation. So much increasing. I reveal an ace four cards into my draw pile. I kept things simple this year. The pink hotel year, I planned for different sun, champagne served poolside, cakes adorned with ribbons of shaved pink chocolate. I had room service dreams, confections the size of my face, burger and fries in a bath. I thought I would wake the next day, still high on the heme from dinner, baptized by loneliness.

CANADIAN GAY PORN SITE

Tao Lin

In August 2009, I got an email from a man named Nasir who worked for a Canadian gay porn site that was starting a series called "hot, brainy boys." He said, "At our last brainstorming session, your name came up over and over again as a model who our viewers would adore the opportunity to see." I'd be paid $5000 for a one day photo/video shoot. I forwarded the email to my friend Zachary, saying,

> should i do gay porn
>
> or whatever this is
>
> seems like i 'must'

Eleven minutes later, he replied

> I donno
>
> I wouldn't, I feel
>
> Dam

Which kind of surprised me. Fifteen minutes later, I replied

> jesus

seems i'm doing it 'no matter what'

seems lucrative/interesting

like one of my 'gimmicks' but more concrete + $5000

I was very active on the internet back then, doing things which detractors called "gimmicks." A year earlier, I'd quit my part-time job at an organic vegan restaurant after earning $12,000 selling shares of the future U.S. royalties of my in-progress second novel. I'd since finished the novel, which was coming out in a year. I wanted to write another book. I imagined writing a novel that began with the porn email and ended with the porn shoot.

Later, in bed at night, I told my then-girlfriend about the porn offer. She didn't respond. I said I felt sad that she wasn't more encouraging. She said she wanted to be encouraging; she just hadn't expected me to say what I did, and so was thinking about it; and she did, in the following weeks, turn out to be supportive and encouraging.

Nasir and I emailed around 20 times over three weeks. "Of particular importance to us is a pressing need to diversify our models," he said. "In 2010, we plan to include a new design and links to anti-erotic-racism websites." I negotiated the payment to $8000. We discussed kill fees and advances. I agreed to be photographed for "an extensive portfolio of all-nude images" and to be filmed "masturbating on a couch, bed, or standing up." At his request, I sent Nasir photos of my erect penis. He called it "beautiful" and said the "strength of my erection" was "compelling."

I thanked him, saying I was flattered and relieved, and he said, "One of the things that the owners and our attorney want to know as they deliberate is whether you have talked to your girlfriend, publisher, and family about doing this." I said I'd told my girlfriend but wasn't going to tell my publisher or family: "My only family in America is my brother, and we rarely talk; my parents live in Taiwan and I've never told them much about my life." He arranged for me to gchat Nate, the site's lead attorney's assistant.

"Hello there Tao," said Nate.

"How are you?" I said.

"I am doing okay. Thanks so much for asking. How are you?"

"I'm good. Can you tell me a little about what concerns the company lawyer has, and what I could do to possibly resolve those concerns?"

"Well, Christina is concerned about 2 things." Christina was the website's lead attorney. "She is a former editor and she has published in her field. Thus, I presume that her concerns arise from her sense of what might damage a literary career as well as liability issues. I think Nasir's idea that we speak was wise. Let me start with a few direct questions that aim to discover your aims in performing for the company. And forgive me, I am not used to chatting and I do hope that my chatting is not too lawyerly and stitled."

"Your chatting seems good so far," I said.

He asked if I'd "performed sexually publicly before."

I said no.

He asked why I was interested in doing it apart from the money.

I typed for ten minutes. I pushed enter: "Money accounts for maybe 35% of the reason. The other reasons include (1) I think it would affect my career in a way that I desire, in that I see my career as something that I want to accomplish outside of the mainstream. I've done many things that I feel have caused the mainstream to avoid writing about me, but they have all been things that I felt weren't harming anyone and also were exciting 'artistically' and interesting to me, in my life, and this would be another thing I view in this way. I feel that this will definitely affect my career in a positive manner, from my perspective, which is one where I take the long view, of 5-10 years, and also one where I think about what I want my life to be like when I'm 50 or 60. I feel doing this will make my career more interesting to people that take an interest in my career and also to myself. I feel that it is inevitable that the mainstream will write about me, if I continue doing what I want, and that when they do write about me I want to be in a position where I can 'do whatever I want' without feeling like something I do might offend someone. (2) I feel that I'm often, or sometimes, 'bored' with my life, and it causes me to do certain things, from taking risks in my books to taking risks on my blog or doing things like getting a tattoo that says 'fuck america,' and I think I always feel better after having done one of those things. I feel I would regret not taking this opportunity, and in that way I feel I 'must' do it."

"I appreciate the length and honesty of your reply. More questions: (1) How do you feel about being associated with a demonstrably homosexual organization? (2) Within 5-10 years do you hope to garner a more mainstream publisher? If so, how do you feel that performing for us will affect such a quest? (3) How do you feel about millions of people seeing your penis, your ejaculation, and you in a sexual light?"

"I feel positive and excited about being associated with a demonstrably homosexual organization. Within 5-10 years I hope to either remain with my current publisher or, more likely, self-publish on a press I started last year. I do not foresee myself pursuing a larger or more mainstream publisher, but wish, even, to make myself even more 'unavailable' to larger publishers. I feel it is more exciting and interesting to gain an audience independently, and that it's less worrisome/stressful to have more control. I feel positive about millions of people seeing me, in that I feel I will become less inhibited and more confident in my normal life. I understand the main page will feature a non nude photo, I think, and that only subscribers would be able to view the nude photos and the video. And I feel comfortable and positive about that."

The homepage would show one or two "preview pictures" that would "indeed show penis and ass and include enticing captions and banners," clarified Nate. "Many gay gentlemen love seeing erect penises and our models in a state of maximum arousal. This entices them to buy a membership. Also, we provide a few short video excerpts for select blogs to write features that get us subscribers. Although our videos and images are DRM'd we cannot control those subscribers who aggregate our pics and spread them around. We live in an incredibly gossip obsessed Western culture and literary blogs and "intellectual gossip" sites like Gawker or Fleshbot have the money and means to uncode and get the pictures and videos."

"I understand that and feel I expect gossip sites to do what you mentioned, and am clear on that, and am fine with that."

"Whew," said Nate. "That was a major concern. These gossip sites are malicious." He asked if I'd "ever been erect or aroused in the company of other males."

I said no.

"At the photoshoot do you think you may be able to get and maintain and erection by masturbating with 2 or 3 male crew members present?"

"Honestly I'm not sure, having not done something like that before."

"When you ejaculate how does your semen direct itself out of your penis? Shooting? Ebbing? Can you masturbate in a variety of positions--standing, reclining, sitting--to make an interesting erotic story?"

"If I have a medium-strong or strong ejaculation it shoots. If it is weak it 'ebbs.' I haven't experimented much with masturbating in a variety of positions. I know I can standing, reclining, and on my stomach."

"I have just one more question for the evening. Would you be willing to audition for this, not in Canada, but in the States? The audition aims to simply see if you can jerk off in the presence of another guy who you do not know."

"Yes, I would, but would ideally want to be advanced some amount of money for that, as it seems sort of like it's a way around the kill fee."

"Do you have any male friends that you might try this out (jerk off in front of him) so you can definitely tell us that you can perform?"

Two days later, I emailed Zachary

would you want to watch me masturbate

the porn people want me to see if i can do it in front of a male

think it'll be harder in front of you than 'strangers'

so if i can do it with you watching i feel i'll be able to do it

I emailed my then-girlfriend telling her what I'd emailed Zachary, and she offered to be there when I masturbated in front of Zachary, if he agreed to it. Zachary and his girlfriend and I lived in the same apartment. The door to my room was always closed because I was allergic to Zachary and his girlfriend's cats. Zachary replied hours later:

could you give me money?

i was thinking maybe one amount if you can't do it, and a higher amount if you can do it

i want to help you, but i feel money would be 'in order,'
kind of

maybe you should think of a percentage of what you will
be getting paid or something

I forwarded the email to my then-girlfriend, saying "jesus." She
pointed out that Zachary hadn't paid me when I cared for his cats
while he was away. She said I could masturbate in front of her if I
wanted. She suggested two of my male friends that I could ask—
Miles and Justin—but I didn't want to ask them. I'd felt comfortable asking Zachary in part because I'd felt that he'd be interested. I
didn't respond to Zachary's email.

Five weeks later, in late September, I got an email from Christina
saying that Nasir and Nate had both gotten H1N1—swine flu—and
that Nasir had visa problems and was "stuck in Denmark" with his
computer and cell phone impounded. "This is the price one pays for
being of Arab descent these days," she added parenthetically. The
audition was delayed "until one of these gentleman returns to us well
or whole."

Two weeks later, Christina emailed again. "For now, I am han-
dling negotiations with you personally," she said. "Here is why. Nate
has a preexisting condition and his H1N1 infection mushroomed
into full-blown pneumonia. He is in critical condition in the hospital. Nasir is still stuck in Europe and we hope to work through his
visa problems and get him back to Canada by Thanksgiving or, at the
latest, Christmas." She offered to serve as my no-fee agent, said she'd
"contact other publications" to "generate other posing work" for me.
I accepted her offer. I said I only wanted photographic work.

Two weeks later, she emailed me, "I am having considerable trouble booking you for just photographic pictorials. If you are willing to

do video, please let me know." I responded the next day: "I am willing to do video. However, can you update me on the status of what Nasir first contacted me about? What is the estimated time of that being able to move forward, do you think? Do you know of any other way I can make money? I'm going to have to get a job soon if I don't find some way to make some money."

She responded ten days later, saying Nasir was still being held in custody in Denmark. "He is our principal video editor so most of the company's work is on hold and we are just updating sites with material from our backlog and archives (and fluffing that it is 'new'). During the American Thanksgiving week I am traveling myself to Denmark to be on the ground, speak with our European attorney and see how Nasir is doing. Nate is still in the ICU but he is doing better." She recommended that I look into burlesque dancing. She wrote a paragraph about how I could do this.

I replied, "I think I'll 'pass" on the burlesque dancing. I'm still interested in posing nude and masturbating on camera for money however."

Three weeks later, on November 18, Christina emailed: "I am very sad to report from Europe that Nasir had been severely beaten while in custody in Prague before being sent to Denmark. I had no idea of the extent of his injuries or that he was physically abused while in custody. Nasir is staying at a trauma center here in Denmark. It will take him time to recover. His jaw is wired shut and the bones in his right hand (which he used to defend himself) have been shattered. I will be in Europe working with the authorities and our immigration attorney until December 11th."

On December 5, Christina emailed saying she'd found work for me at "15K-20K US plus transportation and non-exclusive rights" for a website, which would email me.

A week later, when I hadn't responded to her email yet, she emailed again: "While I am here in Europe, I have discovered that the test results from an intervention came back positive for breast cancer and I have decided that when I return I must take a leave to investigate chemotherapy, radiation, a double mastectomy, or a combination of the above."

She said, "Trying to recruit on your behalf has given me a window into the challenges that Nasir faced and why he was so keen on booking models-of-color. I feel comfortable telling you that the problem that I encountered concern the studios' reluctance to book a model of Asian descent."

She'd "located a recruiter who is directly linked to several online studios who may be able to better assist you further." She said, "I do not know him. This is just a referral. But, by all accounts, he is good. If you want to continue with this, please give him an email or a call. He does recruit gentlemen-of-color."

Her long email ended, "Lastly, I feel strongly that in the event that he cannot book you, then I would take notes about his approach and start your own booking/recruiting endeavor and focus exclusively on finding fresh-faced young guys for online gay porn studios (straight studios usually have in-house recruiters). The money is lucrative if you control your own recruiting business. I will give you pointers if you go this route."

I was somewhat confused by the length and intimacy of her email, by how much she wanted to help me, and by her suggestion that I become a recruiter for online gay porn studios.

Everyone at the company that I'd talked to had seemed to write in a formal, polite, literary manner—with long, interesting sentences—which I found gentle and calming—and had all seemed very generous with their help and time.

I must have been busy with other things, and/or to have lost interest in doing porn, because I didn't respond for a full month, until January 12, when I replied with just two sentences—"I'm very sorry to hear of this news, and sincerely hope that you make a full recovery. I appreciate your continued support and the information in this email."

Ten years later, in January 2021, I saw that the website still existed. It was subtitled "Real Amateur Homemade Gay Porn Videos" and seemed professional. The front page featured photos of naked young men seated on sofas with erections.

THE HOUSE ON THE HILL IN THE COUNTRY

David Fishkind

They had concluded they wanted to move to the country.

They were a young couple and had been living in the city for so long the conclusion risked not coming at all.

They'd met at a bar near an art gallery after an opening three years prior, when they'd still entertained aspirations of becoming artists themselves. Their devotion grew. Their careers went nowhere.

Lately, they'd been unemployed for five and a half months.

The museum where she'd copyedited wall text had closed the same week that the television program for which he'd been nursing a four-year scenic's assistantship ceased production.

At the end of some Thursday, she'd been told she should plan to work remotely from home. Two weeks after, she'd been laid off.

He'd been assured, as soon as filming resumed, he could expect a call. But by then his phone had been on *Do Not Disturb* for three months.

Few continued to anticipate expectations. Most agreed: times were tough.

The couple's circumstances were not unique, nor were they particularly dire. They downloaded the Department of Labor mobile app and claimed weekly benefits. They remained afloat. Their hearts fluttered. They no longer liked to go outside without each other.

They agreed: it was a matter of time.

When they were very honest, they confessed they no longer liked to go outside in the city no matter what.

*

After two months of imitating YouTube yoga vlogger flows, reading *Bleak House* aloud, and failing to make headway on the stoneware collection they'd resolved to throw with the pottery wheel he'd purchased after college, she broke down and ordered an emotional support animal.

The puppy arrived via Sprinter van, retrofitted with a generator and grid of kennels, shivering in Xanax-induced dismay. They brought it into the apartment, where it proceeded to evacuate fourteen hours' worth of waste.

This was an animal that required going outside.

It had never been a large apartment, but they'd never spent so much time in it. The city demanded a vibrant public. Yet amenities for that kept disappearing. Replaced by plywood facades. Cops cracking down on joggers in the park.

Not to mention they'd already had a cat, who took an immediate disliking to the canine. With all their hot blood on top of one another, and without an idea of when restrictions might lift, it seemed only reasonable to covet more space.

They were gloomy, anxious. Their elected officials did not seem concerned as to whether they died or lived, which was more relevant than usual, because people in the city were, in fact, dying at alarming rates.

Perhaps it was out of respect for misfortune. They were hesitant to fantasize. They never said, —We should just leave.

By degrees, they let it slip.

If they quit the municipality he could build a homemade kiln, she hinted. She could finally, he noted, spread out and weave to no limit. They wouldn't have to wait in snaking sidewalk lines to buy twenty-five-pound bags of rice. Shielding their faces. They could plant a modest garden, go on hikes, rake leaves, shovel mud.

Neither had experience living rurally. No more than they'd learned to navigate conditions of civic strife.

They opened windows, blew funnels of smoke at the screens. The air appeared to sink. Sounds of sirens and flash bangs. Helicopters whipping mini doppler effects against the jet stream.

—What do you want to do, they said.

The puppy turned in figure eights. It slept most of the day. When its paws touched dark asphalt, it balked. Muscles spasmed with panic, unable to offer much in the way of emotional aid.

How long could they keep their afloatness from going broke? And what exactly were they hoping to tolerate?

*

She tapped his forearm. Her phone displayed quilting patterns.

A laugh fractured. He shook his head, trying to clear thoughts of derision and acquiesce. It was bad where they were. He challenged her to find someplace more promising, affordable, with a better air quality index.

He claimed to not care what happened. He claimed to be of the mindset that things would return to some concurrence.

Time mattered. He took it as a provocation. She took it as fate.

She filtered through Facebook, craigslist, real estate websites, and texted him links from across the apartment.

He rejected things. Too small to be worth it, too much work or too ugly or he'd search the addresses and point out proximities to questionable powerplants, waste water facilities, too nearby of neighbors, because he didn't want to leave the cold comforts of the metropolis just to be pushed up against some hacking homebody who wanted nothing more than to knock on their door for a cup of gluten-free baking ingredients every other afternoon.

She wasn't discouraged. She sent him a listing for a cabin upstate, on thirty acres, at seventy-five percent the cost of their present rent.

He muttered something about baseboard heat. He walked the length of the apartment, pretended to look out a window. She and the puppy followed the trails his fingers smudged along the glass.

—Okay, he said. —When can we see it?

She called the next morning.

—Hi, she said in a loud, genial way.

She nodded and attempted to get in half-phrases over the hum at the other end of the line. When she hung up her mouth tightened. The cabin had been spoken for by another young couple.

—Jesus, he said. —How long had it been vacant?

—The post was from yesterday. I'll keep looking.

His throat issued an arguably involuntary noise.

She dipped to her knees and hobbled over to where he sat, back rigid, buttocks clinging to the edge of the mattress pushed into the corner of the room. They no longer changed outfits or worried about bathing, sleep, or scheduled meals.

A burning smell emanated. Fast, short blasts erupting, then echoed reports between them and the building across the intersection.

—As my solemn vow, she folded her hands, —I will find us the perfect pastoral sanctuary. We'll leave this place. Forever, should we decide to. We're a family. We'll protect each other. What have we got to lose?

The puppy quivered under the sheets. The cat curled on paint flakes. The young couple agreed: they embraced.

*

The next place she found was in a bucolic valley town of an abutting state.

They scrolled through the photos. The house appeared to sit on the bump of a much larger hill overlooking plain fields, unfurnished and made mostly of wood.

—Isn't it a little…

He trailed off.

—They took them this way because they know what a deal they've got. They're downplaying the place.

—Okay, he said. —Make the call, quick, before we lose it.

But there was no phone number listed. Her first email was short. A simple query for more pictures, and when they could come up for a viewing.

Six hours later, without a response, she wrote again:

My name is Anna and my partner Andrew and I are very interested in the house. Andrew is a ceramicist and I'm a copy editor and we're looking to permanently relocate to the area from the city. We've been looking for a manageable, private home where we can get settled into a slower pace of life. I feel like we'd be an ideal fit. We're a very quiet, low-maintenance couple. Please do let me know if you're interested. The house is quite beautiful. All the best…

He read over her shoulder as she typed the message. Between *house* and *is quite* he added *, from what we can tell,* and pressed the send button before she could alter anything else.

Half an hour later, they received a reply:

Greetings Anna. Thank you for your interest. The house is lovely, though spare, and the setting is pristine. We've had a flurry of responses for this new posting, many of them from the city. For now we're gathering and sorting inquiries. Feel free to add anything about you and Andrew, and we can also try to field key questions at this early stage. Warm regards. –Zeke

—What more could he want you to add?

—I don't know, she said. —I don't want to seem too eager. Let's try and sleep on it, and I can email him back in the morning.

But neither could rest. He kept getting up to reexamine the

listing. It hadn't been up two hours when she'd replied to it.

The photos were taken from confusing angles. The light accentuated dust. It didn't account for a road or address.

She sifted through Google Street Views of the town, zooming in when she thought she spied a corresponding structure, zooming out again and again.

*

She was dissatisfied with her response:

Thanks so much for the quick reply, Zeke! I wish there was something exciting I could tell you about Andrew and myself that would distinguish us! Perhaps we could schedule a time to speak on the phone. We're looking for a minimum year lease. When are you hoping to rent the house?

Six minutes later, she sent an addendum:

we really really love the house and would love to come up to see it as soon as possible. It really is exactly what we've been looking for. Apologies for all the emails!

And when the next afternoon, her inbox bore nothing new, she sent:

Hi Zeke, just following up. We're very eager to set a time to look at the house. Would it be possible to see it this weekend or early next week? We have a few questions about the property and would love to speak with you over the phone or even Facetime/zoom if that's your preference. We are quiet, crafty people without many possessions looking for an affordable spot in a more rural area as we plan to spend the next year preparing Andrew's sculptures for his first solo exhibition. As I mentioned, Andrew is a ceramicist and I'm an editor, as well as a weaver/tapestry maker/ amateur seamstress. Andrew worked for a TV show the past 5 years, but recently decided to pursue art full-time. I also do freelance work for a number of art institutions. We'd be prepared to provide the usual first, last, and security. We have excellent credit and references. If you're look-ing for responsible, respectful, low-maintenance tenants to care for the house, feel free to call or text me at…

Fifteen minutes later, her phone started to vibrate.

*

He watched her face react to the imperious buzz from the phone's other end.

He imagined the voice as rasping and dim, dropping R's and drawing Ah's long as it bounced through the hills, pinging off towers between the states.

Outside, in the city, men wore masks and dug a hole across the intersection. A truck tried to circumvent them and lost a wheel in the process.

—Thank you so much, she said and put her phone atop the doz-ing cat.

Its skin constricted and fur stood on end, then slackened.

—So?

She raised her eyebrows.

—Zeke said we can come the day after tomorrow. He says they've got to fix up the place. Apparently the previous tenants were a real *class act*.

She did air quotes with her fingers.

—And they're not in a rush to fill it. But honestly I think we're the perfect fit. I'm glad I emailed so much. I think that you worked in TV did it. He kept asking about the show.

—What'd you say?

—Just whatever it seemed like he wanted to hear. He kept allud-ing to that actor. I said you two were old pals.

He swallowed.

—I barely know any of them.

—I don't think it matters. We just needed something to stand out.

—Did he have anything to say about my fake exhibition?

—Not really. I don't know if he knows about art. He seems obsessed with celebrity. I'm sorry for lying by the way, I just wanted to cast every line that we could. I think it paid off.

—Zeke, he said.

He nuzzled his face in the puppy's neck. He was not looking forward to walking it. He still hadn't got down the rhythm of putting on the mandated protective equipment.

—And he's okay with pets?

—Damn, she hesitated. —I completely forgot to ask.

*

They debated what to do next.

She figured they could get away with showing up. How better to win over a wary heart than by confronting it with puppy eyes. Downy white fur. That sweet, earthy smell it effused.

He thought it might be worth getting a sense of where the landlord stood on the issue before driving three hours only to be disappointed by some allergy or prejudice or histrionic provision.

—But it looks like the property's part of a farm. What kind of farmer harbors aversion to sweet little mutts?

—I don't know, he said. —Maybe the kind who posts purposefully bad photos to downplay the quality of the house they're trying to rent? Or maybe not. Would it really hurt to call him?

As it turned out, Zeke must have been a fanatic. He droned over the line, and she nodded and gave a thumbs up, the initial root syllables of response words escaping her throat in fits.

When she hung up, she stayed beaming. After phone calls she always experienced the paranoia that the line remained connected, and through a kind of bewitchment she could be seen. That any joking or disparaging thing she might say, think, or wince at would yet be sucked through the earpiece and into the consciousness of whomever had been at its receiving end.

—Well, Zeke loves dogs.

—I could've guessed, he said.

—He used to have Scottish terriers, but they died. He got kind of off on a tangent.

—That's great. But it didn't seem like you managed to bring up the cat…

She sighed.

—No reason to bombard the man with questions. If he's cool with a pup, I can't imagine any brooding objections to a sleepy old kitty.

He tried to imagine Zeke brooding. He couldn't picture him.

—One weird thing, though. He mentioned the *flurry* of responses he's gotten. That's the second time he phrased it like that. But this time it felt like a threat. Like before he was saying they weren't in a rush to choose a tenant. And in his email he said *at this early stage*. But then just now he mentioned the *flurry* of responses. Almost like he was trying to tell us not to bother, or like we shouldn't put all our eggs in his basket. But then he said he was really looking forward to meeting us and the pup, so I don't know what to think.

—That is weird, he said.

—Yeah, but get this. He said he has an old high-fire kiln in his basement. I didn't even touch on ceramics. He just said it like an aside, so clearly he remembers us among everyone else. I still feel good. Zeke's just odd.

He didn't require additional assurance to agree with that. But he felt placated. He trusted her judgment.

They made love that night, and the following morning, and late in the afternoon, as light crawled behind buildings and split, throwing triangles across the intersection in the hot, hissing city, again.

*

The puppy panted in the car's passenger seat. Windows cracked to exchange humidities. He opened a GPS mobile app.

—Wait, he said. —So is he meeting us at the address of the house, or are we meeting him at his address first?

She looked up, hands in tote bag, sifting through granola bars and protective equipment.

—Uh, I'm not sure. I think he lives somewhere else. On the property. He said to meet at the white house with the red door and we could walk over to the house on the hill with him.

—So we'll be sharing an address with Zeke?

—I don't know, she said. —I don't fully know what we're doing. I'm just excited we came to this conclusion. I'm excited we're acting intentionally to improve our conditions.

—I guess I'm confused.

—I know, I know, just hold on, I want to make sure we have everything.

While he drove they listened to a podcast. Two men discussed why feminism was inherently racist over sound bites of airs horns and artillery fire. The puppy slept in a footwell.

—Did you remember your mask?

—Yeah, he said.

—Zeke just emailed to say we need to wear masks and gloves, and if we have glasses that would also be great, but he's less concerned about glasses than the other things.

—Did you bring gloves?

—Yeah, she said. —I keep checking to see if I forgot them, but they haven't gone anywhere.

A digital sign on the highway warned that vehicles with out-of-state plates could be pulled over for random evaluation.

—Why does he want us to wear glasses? I haven't heard anything about glasses during any of this.

—I don't know. He knows we're coming from the city. He's probably just being cautious.

—That's fine, he said. —I just don't get why. Like I'm not mad. Only curious if there might be new info we missed.

Every ten or so miles, another digital sign about being pulled over appeared.

STAY HOME, others said.

FEEL SICK?

There were a lot of cars, though, and they hadn't noticed police lights or sirens. As far as they could see down the highway, the road was even.

*

They took the exit the app indicated and made their way to a narrow road surrounded by tall, dense trees and without a center line.

—Look, she exclaimed.

She held the puppy and rolled down the window so it could stick out its face.

—We're still twenty minutes away.

—I'm excited, she laughed.

The GPS coiled out sparse instructions. They kept looking for roads, then nearly missing the turns, braking at the top of steep gradients. Signage faded, worn by time. Posts bent. Some were missing, and he had to judge, compare with the two-inch LED map, and make his best estimate.

As they cruised over slopes, dodging semi-trailer trucks, which emerged at the crux of hairpin curves, and obtuse-angled switchbacks, internet and cell service dropped out and in. Rays of sun trickled through the verdure overheard.

Some distance off the road, a farm stand caught her eye.

—Hearpy's Farm, she said, pronouncing the first word like *harpy*. —I wonder if that's the same Hearpy as my boss, I mean my ex-boss's family. I've never seen the name anywhere else. Plus I'm pretty sure he grew up around here.

—Good portent, he said.

They came to a dirt road. It appeared to lead to their destination, and, according to the app, culminate in a dead end. They dipped at an abrupt ridge, then climbed again.

He could already imagine the number this habitual trip would do on his brakes. He'd have to learn how and when to shift into the lower gears of the automatic's transmission.

She saw the look on his face and hoped he'd keep his mind open. She had a really good feeling. The puppy licked, alternating between window glass and her chin.

He wondered if he'd have to install chains on his tires come winter.

The road widened. Trees cleared above, and the incline subsided a bit. Rock walls trailed the lush grassy shoulder. Old barns and colonial houses arose every few hundred yards. But for the most part it was open country, undeveloped and untainted. They were kicking up dust. They breathed deep, took in the idyllic bouquet of backwoods.

—There it is.

She pointed, and the white house with the red door materialized through an amber sparkle of pollen and monarch butterflies. The swarm overtook the windshield for a perfect instant.

—Migration season, she said.

*

They parked in front of a rust-colored shed at what seemed like the edge of the property. *Avertissement!*, a sign affixed to its door announced in bold letters.

—Wow, she said. —Seems like they're French speakers.

—What does it mean?

—Like, warning, or caution, but, you know, there's no perfect translation between any languages.

He looked at his phone. It showed one modicum of a bar for making calls. He pulled the parking brake and cut the engine.

She and the puppy got out of the car. Immediately the creature was transformed. Usually too timid to leave her side more than a few feet at a time, it bolted, tail lashing ferocious, across the dirt road into a vast meadow and lifted its leg.

Then it squatted with glee. In lieu of a plastic bag, she had to resort to one of the gloves. She turned it inside out and, coming up short in her cursory search for somewhere to deposit it, slipped the makeshift latex waste vessel under the passenger seat.

She hadn't even had time to secure the puppy's leash. When she caught up to it, it was investigating a smoldering stump in the weeds.

The smell was hypnotic. Sour and peppery and alluring as it was nauseous. Nothing around suggested disturbance. She wondered how or why it alone might have burned.

He was messing with something in her tote bag. Arrayed in mask, baseball hat, sunglasses, and gloves. She realized she wasn't wearing any of the agreed-upon accoutrements.

She and the puppy trotted back to the car. He had her phone out and was attempting to make a call.

—No service, he said.

She tightened the leash's tether, about to check the phone herself, he was famously incompetent with tech, when the *Avertissement!* sign began to rattle, and the shed door opened.

They assumed the woman, who'd introduced herself as Eunice, was Zeke's wife. But Eunice hadn't, they later agreed, going over the day's events, ever actually elucidated the nature of her relationship to the landlord.

She remembered apologizing for being caught off guard, for prioritizing the puppy, for being irresponsible and disrespectful of the prearranged etiquette.

He thought she'd overdone it. Eunice, for one, wasn't wearing a mask, gloves, or glasses. Plus she'd barely left the area surrounding their vehicle.

No damage could possibly have been done in those few moments. And so prosaic a faux pas could not possibly have accounted for their failing to procure a lease on the house on the hill in the country.

But they would speculate for weeks. This had been her sole opportunity for a first impression. She beat herself up with convictions and critiques.

He had been friendly. He'd waved, and at the last moment refrained from the impulse to stick out his hand.

—How are you, he yelled, overcompensating for the sake of the mask.

—Zeke's occupied at the moment, Eunice said. —He'll meet with you after you look at the house. Go on up. As you can see, there's a driveway you'd use if you happened to live in the place, but don't worry about that. Just take the path, then turn around the way. Most people prefer the back entrance.

—Thanks, they said.

—Take as long as you need. Don't rush looking around. Get a feel for things. That house has energy. Try to imagine if you could really stand to live…

Eunice trailed off. She looked behind her, into the dim opacity of the shed, then closed the door with both hands.

—There, the woman uttered.

*

The back door was locked. He put his face to the sidelight. Particles drifted through the air inside.

They walked to the front, where the weatherstripping had peeled away and furled in the dry, warm breeze. The door was spartan, definitely antiquated, and it gave with some shouldering.

Tears started in her eyes the moment she entered.

Her father had been an architect.

She ran a hand down the heavy wood frame. Dragged the toe of her sandal along worn yet sturdy floorboards.

—This is where I want to be, she sniffed.

He was surprised by the visceral aspect of his own reaction. The house loomed with essentiality.

Soon her tears luminesced through a broad grin. She'd been right in her hypothesis. The photos from the listing didn't just minimize the house's aura, they debased it.

The main room was economical, though not an inch could be described as cramped. Instead, it was designed with exacting efficiency. An acute sense of flow and volition. It gave the impression of having been arranged by ordainment, not unlike the effect of a well-executed public park, or feng shui.

Large windows broke up the duskiness of the wood. A provident ledging extended from the sills, drawing across, uninterrupted, the perimeter of the room, but for the cast iron wood stove, which burgeoned from the center wall of the far end, hemmed in by conservative safeguards made of stone, which they assumed were indigenous to the property.

A large butcher block divided the rest of the space. Fixed up against a stylish, though not aggressively state-of-the-art, oven and gas range. On first glance, they didn't even notice the refrigerator. Thus rounding out the room's empyrean sensation.

The rest of the house proved equally ideal. It was no bigger than they would ever have use for, nor too small as to feel they couldn't get away from one another.

There was a washing machine in a mudroom with a clothesline running the length of it. And another, accessible just out the window, from which he could see a lean-to stocked with treated, pre-split firewood.

A sizeable bedroom surveyed the rolling landscape, left behind by glacial melting, the pounding of mammoths.

Built-in shelves graced the hallway's width, as well as the closets and pantry.

Finally, up a slender ladder, they could access a spacious and light-flooded loft.

They lay on the wood breathing. At the foot of the steps, the puppy gazed up longingly.

He broke their rapt silence.

—We can't let this place go.

—I know, she gasped. —I feel it.

—We have to be confident. Assertive. We have to say, we want to rent your house, this is where we want to live, what can we do to sign an agreement today, no hesitation.

*

His hands sweated in the gloves. It was early afternoon, and the sky was bare luster, no clouds.

He took the puppy by its leash and exited through the front of the house, careful to wrap the weatherstripping around the doorknob so it wouldn't peel farther off.

—Are you ready?

—Hold on a second.

She went back inside. He heard her fumble with something. An unfamiliar sound emanated. A low guttural groan. It took him a moment to realize it came from the puppy. Then it burst in frantic yaps, snarling and forlorn, building to the full, bold barks of a much matured dog.

In the four months since she'd ordered it, he couldn't recall the puppy ever out-and-out barking. Any errant, instinctual yelp had always been effortlessly subdued.

But outside the house on the hill in the country, the puppy conducted itself with beast-like passion. Tugging and squirming and hollering. Its acrid tones ricocheted through the atmosphere.

In the constant reminiscences that followed, attempting to comprehend why they hadn't been granted their rightful claim as tenants, they agreed: nothing had ever caused the puppy to behave or make another fuss as it had in that moment on that day.

Because it persisted for less than a minute. Until she scrambled to his and the animal's side.

—What was all that?

She was shaking.

—I don't know, he said. —What were you doing?

—I just wanted to give the basement a peek. Did you see that floor hatch?

—Sure, he shrugged. —Anything interesting?

—Not really. It was unfinished. More like a crawl space. I couldn't see much, and I didn't want to drop down. It's a good amount of space though. We could store boxes or luggage or whatever there.

—When we move in, he said.

—When we move in.

She hugged him and the puppy, who'd returned to its coy, aloof temperment upon the click of the latch in the doorframe.

*

Eunice was still by the shed when they came down the hill. They waved, and she squinted, raising a hand over her brow to block the sun. She adjusted the *Avertissement!* sign and stepped back, crouching to get a better look.

—Hi, they said.

—I'll go get Zeke, Eunice answered. —What did you all think?

—Well, we want to rent your house, he said.

—Oh?

Eunice laughed.

—So sure already?

—We are, she said.

—What can we do to make a commitment today?

—Take a seat by the garden. We've got it all set up nice, and Zeke'll be with you to go over brass tacks in a jiffy. Our hot water went out, and he just can't seem to make sense of it.

—Andrew's hopeless with mechanics, she teased.

He brought a glove to his mask to make sure it was fitted correctly. Eunice remained stooped. She put her hands on her knees, then reached one out to the puppy. It examined the digits, kept its distance, and snorted. Then backed off, twisting itself in the leash.

—Sorry, she said. —He's still pretty shy with people. But he's great with other animals. We've only had him a few months. He came from a farm. I think he can sense this is where he wants to be.

—He's not the only one, Eunice smiled and pushed herself to her feet. —You make yourselves comfortable. Can I get you anything?

—Oh no, we're fine, he said.

—What about Fido? He want some water? What's his name by the way?

—Houdini, she said.

—Be careful. You might end up with a self-fulfilling prophecy.

—I'd be more concerned if he showed any interest in being more than five feet away from me.

—You never know, Eunice said. —A place like this can cause all kinds of excitement. I'd hate for him to get lost, or, Hades forbid, there've been known to be predators that come down from the mountains.

—We'll make sure to keep him on a tight lead.

—I'm sure you would. But let's not get ahead of ourselves. I'll get Zeke.

*

Later, the young couple went over the garden in detail. Perhaps they thought it held a clue in its arrangement. One that could explain why they weren't bestowed the privilege of basking in its splendor ever again.

A small wrought iron table with a frayed lace runner was prepared on the patio, with two matching chairs near it, on the side of the white house with the red door. On the table rested a pitcher of water. And two more chairs, different ones, were positioned about eight feet from the other end of the table, and spread far apart.

The garden looked scorched. Flowers and weeds overgrown and dried up. A deer fence surrounded it with minor failings and mendings and bends in the mesh.

Further along the hill, where, if not for trees and shadow, they'd be able to make out the little house for rent, another fence, this one staunchly secured with long barb razor wire curling at its top, framed what appeared to be five wooden boxes. There, another sign announced, *Ne Pas Toucher!*

Every other direction revealed georgic scenery. Immaculate

vistas of golden hay bales and rich, healthy fields of green.

They brought the chairs on their side of the table a little closer to each other and tied the puppy's leash to one of the legs.

She stood admiring the view, imagining it when fall hit. Foliage glowing in ombre shades. She tried to tighten a glove, pulling at the wrist, but it broke, and she was riffling through her tote bag for an extra when she detected faint movement in the meadow across the street.

—Oh my god, she said. —Are those goats on our property?

—They'd better be, a voice said.

They turned to see a middle-aged-looking man wearing a shimmering headlamp. He brandished a stack of four glasses and was smoking a hand-rolled cheroot. He coughed twice through the haze.

—Rather, they'd better be on my property.

He placed the glasses on the table and slid two in their direction. An ejection between a hack and a giggle issued from the space made by the cigar and his otherwise unmasked, clenched teeth.

Eunice stepped out the red door, hands on her hips.

—Sorry for the wait, the man said. —But I think I've got everything up to speed. The most important lines are prepared for rehearsal at least. I mean, the water lines... Are repaired... For the... Housing... The housing retreat.

The young couple nodded.

The man said, —I'm Zeke.

*

He asked if they needed anything. They shook their heads. Zeke insisted they all drink some water.

They agreed: it was time to do whatever was asked of them.

The man sniffed the pitcher. He ran the inside of a wrist across his forehead and scowled at the woman in the doorway.

—Eunice, Zeke called. —How long's this water been sitting?

—Just since they pulled in.

—It's gone bad.

Zeke rubbed the bridge of his nose. He apologized.

—I'm sorry, I'll get you fresh water. It won't be a minute.

The light from the headlamp caught him in the eye as Zeke swung around and back toward the main house.

He winced and looked at her. She was half-sitting, half-out-of-the-chair by his side, struggling to fit a new glove over the ripped one and her palm, which was slick with perspiration.

—Eunice, Zeke said. —Come down and tell 'em about the accommodations.

—Why don't you tell them, she grunted.

—'Cause I'm getting the fresh water drink.

He marched past her. The woman hesitated. Then she moved through a dramatic curtsy and waltzed down the slate pathway from the front steps to the table on the patio, where the puppy panted compulsively, its tongue hanging to the ground.

—So, Eunice said.

—Your home is beautiful, she answered. —What year was it built?

—I'm not entirely the best one to ask, the woman looked over her shoulder. —But a long time back. Zeke was born here. His parents were from the city, like you two.

She smiled.

—They were political folks. Maybe too political for urban life. They came up here to start some kind of colony. Primarily theater-related, but they filmed movies as well. They never really took to agricultural culture. For a long time they leased out the land, and then Zeke sold some of it since it's been in his name. Mostly we prefer to keep it as is.

She looked over her shoulder.

—We're thrilled at the prospect of moving here, he said. —I've got a checkbook in the trunk of my car. We'd be more than happy to leave a deposit. Or even go over the asking price, if that would make any difference.

—To me, Eunice said, pretending to act surprised.

—Or Zeke, he said. —Whatever you guys would want.

—We get quite a bit of snow, the woman said.

—And the goats are all yours, she asked.

—Goats, Eunice repeated. —Everything else. Zeke's very lucky. And we've been lucky enough to have such… Tasteful tenants. But we only cover the first four snowplows of every season. The rest you'd have to pay for yourselves.

—That makes sense, he said.

—There he is.

Eunice shot up the path and switched off Zeke's headlamp. They carried the pitcher together, as if it were a great onus, and Eunice whispered in Zeke's ear the way back to the table.

—So you all like the place?

Zeke chewed the cheroot. It had gone out.

—It's beyond like, she said. —I don't know how to explain the emotional reflex it set off in me.

—You're not the only ones, Eunice said.

—Well, he said. —In the immediate future, we'd like to be.

—Did I happen to mention the flurry of responses we've gotten, Zeke said.

—You have, she said. —And I know you're still in the early stage of finding a renter, but…

—Early, Eunice interrupted.

—Suppose, Zeke said, brushing a knotted hand against the woman's cheek. —Sometimes these things require rigorous pre-production. We like the idea of doing more cleaning, getting a sense of the scope of our prospects. And yet, other times…

Zeke poured water in their glasses. They had to stand to get to the table, and they were careful to keep their distance. Zeke poured water in Eunice's glass and his own. He inhaled thoughtfully before raising it to his lips.

—So you came all the way from the city just to see our humble plot?

They nodded.

—Why don't you tell us a little about yourselves while we've got you here then.

—Well, as I'm sure you're aware, she began. —Things are pretty uneasy in the city.

—To be certain, Zeke said. —Eunice, did you ask if Houdini wants water? I feel like a sadist quenching my thirst in front of the pup.

—I asked, Eunice said.

—Did she ask?

—Uh, I mean, we got kind of off track.

—I'll go grab a bowl.

—Wait, Eunice said. —Let me do it.

—No, no. Just be a minute.

He charged to the red door before anyone could stop him.

—So, um…

She had to sneeze, but she was afraid of what would happen. She tried to swallow. That, however, only made it worse, and she collapsed with her mask on the inside of her elbow.

Her shame was startling. He sensed it.

—We're artists, he said. —Anna is an incredible sewer and designer and tapestry maker, as well as a professional editor. I studied ceramics. And I won't pull any punches, we were both laid off right at the beginning of when things got tense. That said, we were well taken care of when we did work, and we have considerable savings and good credit and we've collected a fair amount from unemployment. We're totally solvent. The rent on the listing is, like, half what we're used to paying.

—How exactly do you make money now, Eunice said.

—Andrew has a solo show coming up this time next year, she chimed in, recovering. —He's being self-effacing, but it could be big. I mean, it will. He got represented by a major gallery, and his sculptures are seriously inspired.

—Zeke told you we've got a working kiln in the basement?

—I mean, he laughed. —You guys ran an artists' colony, right? You know how it is. This stuff is P.O.D. Paid on delivery. In the meantime, I'd be happy to show you a bank statement.

—That's not what that means, Eunice said.

—What, he asked.

—And am I to understand…

Zeke had reappeared. He searched for her eyes. They exchanged notions of stress.

—That you, Andrew, have been working in television?

—It's true, he said. —But it's not really where my heart…

—Can you tell me a little more about that? I've always been highly intrigued by the performing aspect of the arts.

—Oh, it's not glamorous. I mostly deal with sets and props rentals, keeping odds and ends in order. It's not like I'm responsible for doing makeup over anyone's scars or getting behind-the-scenes gossip or anything lurid.

—I'll bet you have some juicy stories.

He looked at her. She raised her eyebrows.

—Maybe, he said. —But there'll be plenty of time to tell tales around the fire pit, right?

He smiled. He'd just noticed the pit by the untended garden, and was proud of his ability to evade Zeke's prying, and without giving away the stark pointlessness that had been his job, his art career, his self in the city.

—What we really want, she said. —Is to leave some of that old life behind us. The grind was great, but we aspire to something more sustainable. More space. Fresh air. I was hoping to get into small-scale herb and vegetable farming.

—Hey, the land is ripe. *We* certainly haven't exhausted the soil. Some of our tenants from time to time get into it. Deep down in the dirty. But I've always been more focused on aesthetics. I was disappointed when the studio didn't take off. We had quite a guild at one time. Almost got a grant that would've provided funds for intensive workshops, biannual runs, reviews, victims from all over the world. Stoical writers, long-suffering actors, real professional types. But stuff kept getting in the way. And now we're old guards ourselves. Isn't that right?

Eunice stared into the distance.

—Well, if you're interested in aesthetics, I don't think you could've picked a better place if you tried, she said.

—We didn't pick it, Zeke said. —My parents did.

—Eunice told us. They were into politics?

—The show must go on, Eunice sang.

They laughed.

Zeke grimaced.

—If you're not happy with the arrangements they provided, you're welcome to leave any time.

Eunice spat on the patio. At once, it began to evaporate. The puppy, water bowl emptied, made a move to lap at it.

—Your home is beautiful, she said. —What year was it built?

—Honestly, who cares, Zeke said.

They let that sink in.

—You wouldn't happen to know, she paused. —I saw a sign for Hearpy's Farm on our way in. My old boss, from the museum, where I worked before all this…

She put her hands up, as though a gesture could give their lives context.

—His name is Hearpy. I think his family is from around here, but further east. Do you think there's a connection?

—Is your old boss a fascist, Eunice asked.

—No, she said.

—Then it's probably not the same.

Zeke relit his cigar.

—She's just mad because the gal's dad called us hippies thirty years ago. But Jude Hearpy's as sweet as they come.

—Their family hunted witches, Eunice said.

—That's right, Zeke laughed through a plume of smoke.

The young couple were smokers. They felt pangs in its presence.

—Four hundred years ago. I think they knew Increase Mather. The Hearpy family was renowned as vicious cult murderers. They came to our end of the state because they were afraid, after the madness abated, that they'd be accused of undue cruelty and strung up to the stakes themselves. They cleared this land, and they founded the farm, and I don't think they bothered anyone since. Except for they did call some of our old friends queers. It's interesting to hear you pronounce their name the same way. Perchance there is a connection. Wouldn't that be great?

The water in the pitcher was gone. The puppy scraped its teeth against the leg of the chair. Sunlight rippled, and the masks felt like they were dissolving, still hooked to the young couple's faces.

—I'd be happy to leave his name and number as a reference, she said.

—Please.

—Zeke, Eunice said.

The woman pulled at her ear. Zeke frowned.

—I just think this place would be perfect for us, he said. —I'm maybe a little selfishly interested in the kiln. And I'm not sure of your parents' political affiliations, but I'd be remiss not to mention that

Anna was on the bargaining committee to unionize the museum she worked at. They had ninety-five members before stuff got bad.

—That's something to be proud, Zeke started.

—They were anarchists, Eunice broke him off mid-speech.

—Well, that's not far from the kind of ideals we adhere to.

—I was wondering about your bumper stickers, Eunice sneered. —Pretty commendable. We wouldn't find any Christian right ones underneath, were we to peel them off?

—If you did, he said. —You wouldn't be the only ones nonplussed.

—You wouldn't be the only ones, either.

Zeke rubbed the bridge of his nose. He removed a handkerchief from his pants pocket, blew into it, and wiped his mouth.

—I'll get you all some popsicles.

—Oh no, that's okay, we're fine, they replied.

—You look like you need popsicles. They're gluten-free.

Zeke's chair capsized.

When he had disappeared into the main house, the woman righted his seat and leaned toward the young couple.

—I wish I could hold your hands right now, Eunice said. —I want you to know, you're both very sweet, and if you don't get the lease, please don't think it has anything to do with who you are. You're virtually paragons. Don't doubt that for an instant.

Zeke returned with two popsicles, unwrapped and beginning to melt.

He was grateful to be wearing gloves, but he didn't know what to do with his mask. She dropped hers off one ear and delicately suckled. He didn't like sweets. He wasn't sure if he could afford to resist.

—We don't trust anyone, Eunice said.

—She means politically, Zeke said.

—We like the doctor. His voice is Jewish, but his face isn't.

They busied themselves with their frozen treats.

—This nation has just gotten so impossible to participate in. The people are disgusting, but I have a feeling people are disgusting no matter where you visit. Have you heard, for example, what kinds of things they eat in the Orient?

She stared at her popsicle. He was stunned, but he felt they were getting closer. Eunice was opening up. He almost nodded.

—Don't say that, Zeke said.

—I know you know what they eat.

Eunice spat again.

—Anyway, Zeke sighed. —We only cover the first four snowplows of every season. The rest you'll have to pay for yourselves.

—That should be fine, she said.

—They *would* pay, Eunice hissed.

—You know how to work a wood stove?

—Constantly, he said.

—Other'n that, things are pretty straightforward. We'll share a few cords with you, but you'll owe us. The well is on your electric bill, but we typically end up covering thirty-three percent of those costs, so that'll be removed from your rent statement quarterly. The washing machine can be removed. We didn't install it, it belonged to a former… Lodger. But we don't really approve. We're environmentalists. We handwash everything. We recommend you do too. And don't go anywhere near the apiary, of course. We put up the electric razor wire fence after bears got into it. Plus we've got to be careful of the wax and honey stockpiled in the shed. You've seen the signs, I presume.

—You speak French, she proclaimed.

—No, Eunice said. —Our daughter got us those. She's been stuck in Marseilles through this whole ordeal, if you can believe it.

—Do you have any other children?

Eunice and Zeke examined each other.

—We're environmentalists too, she said.

—Thank you, Zeke answered. —So you can leave us your references, and we'll let you know when we make a decision.

—Well, okay, that's great, um, but...

She looked at him.

—We were really hoping to put something firm down today, he said.

—You wouldn't be the first to tell us that.

—Have many others made the trip to see the place?

—Many, Eunice said.

—But I thought, he started.

—We're truly eager to live here, she said.

—Then distinguish yourselves, Zeke seethed, his face folding into a theretofore irreconcilable glower. —Give me reason. Demonstrate your worth. Why you? You two. Why here? Why this? Why now?

—We're ready to put our entire souls into the house, she said. —I've been operating under a feeling of fate, from the moment I came upon the listing. And everything you've shared with us today has only heightened that. The history of this place, its whole vibe. It's so in line with our values and goals. It's undeniable. Kismet. And all your ways of doing things, we'll defer to and uphold as if they were our own. I think I speak for both of us when I say we'll make them our own.

She turned to him. He was nodding, spellbound.

—We're more than happy to help you around your property, she continued. —With repairs, the garden, whatever. We've got nothing but time, and we're committed to reshaping our lives. I'm asking you to trust us. With so much uncertainty in the world right now, we need something to count on. Something to dedicate ourselves to. We're receptive to change, malleable, quick on the uptake. We relish a good challenge, and we're not flakes. Even if we are a bit green. Our word means something. Any contract we enter into, we do so with sincerest devotion.

Zeke tilted his head in Eunice's direction.

—So young, the woman preened. —You haven't begun to know the meaning of your *entire* souls.

—We're ready to try, she said.

—The world is always uncertain, Eunice answered.

From deep below, a swell of warmth and rhythm. The pounding of mammoths, she thought.

—Sounds to me like the makings of a hit, Zeke snickered.

Wind washed through the idylls.

—I guess the only question I haven't asked, he said. —So it's great you're cool with Houdini, but I was wondering, what if, down the line, we might also want to bring a cat…

Nobody moved.

—I mean, like, because I've had a cat, but lately, like right now I mean, I've been sharing it with a friend. But I, I mean, if we were to happen to get the chance to rent the house from you, if I wanted to also bring along the cat to…

Zeke shook his head. The cheroot fell to the patio, and he put his face in his hands, the backs of which seemed to have grown remarkably, suddenly hairy.

—We cannot, Zeke suspired through stiff fingers.
—Unfortunately. Abide any cat ownership on the premises.

—No cats, Eunice triumphed.

—Oh, that's okay.

Something rolled in his gut. He wanted to leave this place.

—Like I said, I share it. It's not exclusively ours. It's not, like. It's not even with us right now.

—We've had terrible trouble with cats, Eunice said.

—I'm so sorry to hear that.

—Did you know they can contract and spread the virus?

—It's really no big deal.

—And the smell, Eunice gagged.

—I'm sorry, Zeke muttered. —We really can't abide cats.

—Please, please. No need to apologize.

She turned to him, looking for help. But he was at sea. The cat was his friend. He would mourn it forever when they moved to the country.

—We really love the house, she said.

—Well if that poses no problems, terrific, Zeke bounced back. —I'll get you a pad and paper and you can write down your references and social security numbers and we'll check out your credit scores and everything that can be managed will be managed straight away.

The man tarried in the main house a while, but they were tired of talking. They were tired of watching Eunice stare off absentmindedly spitting. She was imagining the material for the curtains she'd cut.

—My dad was an architect, she said when Zeke returned.

—Terrific, Zeke said. —You all really are tempting folks. It's been such a pleasure to meet you.

—He built the house we lived in, in the city, but it's gone now.

—My friends and I built that house on the hill more than thirty years ago. In the seventies. When the guild was at its peak. Things were different. We didn't know what we were doing. We didn't know what was going on with the world. We sourced the wood. We worked together. We had a lot of fun building that house.

—What happened to your father's, Eunice said.

Zeke turned to the couple.

—I'm sorry. The lady lacks boundaries, but I'll let you in on a secret. That butcher block came from the city. We pulled it off a corner in the restaurant district. Yeah, things were different in the seventies. Not like now. You could get away with anything. When did times get so tough?

—Speaking of time, he said, toiling to work the pen through the limitations of his gloves. —Do you have an estimate for when you'll make a decision regarding tenants?

Zeke took the paper and studied the reference with the name of the television program next to it.

—Wow. So this gal knows a bunch of celebrities and hotshots, huh? Production manager for film and television. I'll bet she's on personal terms with the likes of James Franco.

—I mean… No more than the rest of us?

—Wow, Zeke said.

—Tonight, Eunice said.

—I'm sorry?

She barely heard herself ask the question. Goat dreams dancing behind her eyes.

—Tonight, Eunice repeated. —That's when we'll have our decision made by.

*

His hands shook on the wheel. The puppy snored. It contemplated chickadees and meadow romps. She texted her references, making sure they expected a call from the landlord.

—Oh my god, she said.

—What?

—James Hearpy says someone already called.

—What happened?

—The call lasted less than five minutes. Says he spoke to a nice-sounding woman and gave us a *glowing* review.

She did air quotes again.

He turned on the radio, then turned it down so it was almost silent. Just a hum to match the road sounds. His hand went to his face. His mask was off, but it still itched. He didn't think he'd ever worn one for such a continuous stretch.

—It seems really good, she said. —They're calling people immediately.

—I'm nervous, he said.

—So am I. Do you still like the house? Do you still want to live there? They were eccentric, but ultimately I think they were sweet. I think we could get used to them. And with everything going on, I really don't think they'd bother us.

—I love the house. I'm just sad about the cat.

—The cat is an issue, but I'm glad you handled it the way you did. I don't think they suspected anything. And anyway, we can always bring her in in secret.

—We'll have to, he said.

—It's not like they'd ever know. And if they did find out, it'd be months down the line. What are they going to do then, kick us out? We'll have some stupid altercation, and it'll be over. Don't worry. We'll find a way.

—I'm not going to leave her behind. What could they possibly have against cats?

—Who knows. They probably had a bad experience a long time ago and aren't willing to take another chance. Maybe a cat really stunk up the place. But I don't think they got as fixated as you're fearing. They're calling our references. If they really believed the cat was a dealbreaker, would they go through the trouble?

She had a point, and he always trusted her.

—I think this is the beginning of a very exciting time for us. It's natural to be anxious. But we're taking a huge step. We've been stagnating. Now is our chance to prosper.

His phone vibrated.

—Can you read that, he asked.

She couldn't remember his password. She didn't want him to think she didn't care about him. She just didn't care about passwords.

She tried a handful, too embarrassed to ask, then got locked out for five minutes.

—What's wrong?

—I couldn't remember your password, she said.

When she got it open, she laughed. She held up the screen so he could see the length of the text.

—I guess Zeke really does think he can get something out of you. According to your ex-boss, he monologued for fifteen minutes. Even invited her up to visit. He suggested she bring the cast and crew.

—Jesus, he said. —You see what I meant about the gluten-free neighbor stuff, though? I just hope that popsicle didn't have corn syrup in it. I'm allergic to corn syrup.

But he was laughing too. For what felt like the first time in months, his lungs expanded, and he took a deep, satisfying, cathartic breath.

Then flared his nostrils.

—Wait, what smells like shit?

*

As they were approaching the apartment, Zeke called to ask if she could text screenshots of their credit scores. The man was having trouble with the internet.

He pulled over, she cracked the door, flung the waste glove to the curb, and they navigated to their banks' mobile apps.

That was around five.

When nine p.m. rolled around and they hadn't heard anything, she called back.

This time the woman answered. Eunice said Zeke was busy showing the house to another prospective tenant.

—Did he say anything about our credit information?

Eunice said she wasn't sure, but she'd let him know they'd

checked in.

An hour later, Eunice called to let them know she was so sorry, it had been the most difficult decision they'd ever had to make about the house on the hill, the young couple really was the most exemplary of possible occupants, but they'd decided to give dibs to the first person who'd contacted them about renting it.

She alluded to the fact that he was a single man, and, as expected, he was ready to sign on at once, so he had.

Eunice wanted her to know they were so sorry.

That's when she'd started to cry. He'd watched her face through the call. He'd known it was hopeless from the quality of her second response word:

—Oh.

*

Their initial reaction was: what could you do?

The single man had beaten them to the punch, and had been rewarded deservedly. She hadn't responded until the post had been up for close to two hours. They'd been eating lunch or something. She'd been away from the computer.

She blamed herself.

He blamed the cat.

He was certain its acknowledgment had been their undoing. What kind of people took such a stance, though? People who lived on farms, even if they weren't fond of them, must concede to a feline utility in hunting pests, not to mention general camaraderie. Goats stink up places far worse than cats. They hadn't banned goats from their property.

Nonetheless, it didn't take long to change their tune. Something had been fishy from the start. Remember, the landlord kept dropping hints like they shouldn't get too excited. In fact, hadn't Zeke implied as much the last time they'd talked before making the trip? Almost like he'd been trying to tell them not to bother.

But he'd liked them, they thought. How long Zeke had monopolized his former boss's time suggested earnest investment on his part. Some promise of constancy. Or at least a nod toward their rapport.

They'd brought so much to the table. They'd performed about as faultlessly as anyone could given the circumstances. They'd even preserved their protective equipment when it was clear Eunice and Zeke weren't attached to the protocol.

Besides, what kind of an excuse was it that the first person who reached out about a rental listing got the prize? Since when was that how these things worked? Not then or two hundred years earlier. Nor anything else, for that matter. One chose the preferred, ideal tenant, and that's who signed the lease.

So they must not have been as good a fit as the single man Eunice had cited, difficult as that was to believe.

*

Unless, and this was where their speculations really took off, it wasn't an issue of an even playing field, or even a playing field, in the sense of fair competition, at all.

He pointed out that she'd only ever communicated with Zeke right up to the moment they'd pulled in front of the shed off the dirt road across the street from the meadow. From then forward, it had been clear, despite Zeke's role as property owner, Eunice was the de facto director of the affair.

She couldn't deny it. The bait and switch was near imperceptible, but the experience had been unnerving.

—Zeke didn't even call us back, he said. —After all that. She did.

And remember the way Eunice had interrupted everything

and said for them not to take it personally? The way he saw it, she'd already determined they weren't getting the house long before they'd arrived. She'd probably promised it to someone else in a backroom deal. Perhaps to a relative Zeke was less than fond of. Or maybe they'd posted it on Facebook and their kid in France had sent it to her friend, and before Zeke could intervene, Eunice had consented, and the whole thing had been set in stone, even if Zeke resented the decision being made without him. Even if he'd tried to repudiate it.

—Then again, he said. —Why would Zeke have allowed us to travel all that way if we didn't have a fair shot? He had to have known from your interactions we'd want the house.

—Now that you mention it, she said. —Eunice sounded pretty drained on the phone. I got the sense there'd been a disagreement. You know the way an argument hangs over you after it's over? My guess is Zeke did want us, but she didn't. For whatever reason. It was her final word.

They entertained states of denial. They went back and forth about appealing to Zeke directly.

They slept on it.

In the clarity of morning, however, they gave up. They didn't think Eunice would've called unless she'd been deadset against renting to them. She'd dug their graves before they could raise a hand in protest. Before they could even defend their claim.

Because the house had been theirs, rightfully. The young couple agreed: there was no way the single man could've made a more model denizen.

They imagined what kind of a man he could be. Probably Zeke and Eunice's daughter was an international banker. This guy worked in finance, and would spend the whole winter alone, too lazy to chop wood, instead resorting to the electric burners, and racking up enormous bills to stay warm.

They mocked him. He spoke only in dividends. He'd have no

use for the kiln. He'd never stay up late swapping stories or running old lines with Zeke. He'd be shifty, awkward, sullen.

They despised him. It had been them. They were not the ones to blame. They privately questioned this.

Then resigned to ceaseless doubt and agitation. She said she'd find the perfect place. From the window, he watched the men dismantling buildings. The city glowed green in their hate.

*

Would he have been happy to know he was vindicated? Because he'd been right. The cat had proved their true bane.

Indeed, Eunice had harbored reluctance about renting to a couple. That the girl's father seemed dead was a plus. But they both seemed well-loved. They'd have friends up to visit. Loose ends. Presences. Fuss.

Yet for all her misgivings, she very likely could have been convinced, and caved to Zeke's will, he was so animated at the prospect of having established screen actors involved in the campaign, and who could blame him, he had passion, and a long time had passed since he'd gotten to act on it. She empathized, and she loved him, she really did.

Had it not been for the reference to the cat, categorically, she *would* have been persuaded. It was his family's farm, after all, and his good fortune to share with her as he pleased, nuptial agreements having still served significantly more patriarchal ends when she'd deigned to tie the noose.

She scowled at her platitude.

Yes, all the earthly possessions and habituations she'd ever know may legally be his. But was it not also her stomach?

She could not abide cat. Dog, fine. She'd deal. But she would not stoop to feline flesh. Not after all the sinuous ribs she'd picked her teeth with through the ages. Their fetid fecal hoarding habits. Exclusionary diets of diseased vermin. The breeding grounds that were their mouths, claws, limbs, and innards. The way they draggled their corruptive sacs, relentless.

She was well past retiree-aged, not that she'd ever worked. Still, she'd been firm: she was retired from cat.

This had been their agreement since the turn of the century. He was welcome to argue his case, but you don't throw out hard rules for a chance to chain Saint Elmo's belt around James Franco's waist.

Some things take priority. They were environmentalists. So were the young couple, presumably. They'd have to understand. Waste not, want not. Any animals of prospective occupants would inevitably end up theirs. And how many dogs and cats was one meant to take in every season?

Eunice had had her fair share of pets, and she was sick of it. There was enough to keep track of without having to foster compassion for indolence. The goats made milk. Ensuring their lives was plenty responsibility.

The single man had arrived thirty minutes after the young couple had departed. He came with no baggage, no friends, no critters, no family. He even said he was thinking of getting rid of his phone. In his car's passenger seat, a typewriter sat perched.

He was a writer, he'd said. Probably as full of it as those artist kids. Who could admonish him? Who wouldn't have lied for a chance to live in their house on the hill in the country?

She hadn't felt great about misrepresenting the situation, but unless her inner-polygraph had failed her after so many years, the young couple had set the precedent.

And sure, they'd been disappointed, but disappointment was temporary. If only she could tell them he'd saved both their lives with that offhanded comment.

The cat. She cackled. She had no one to tell.

She looked out the window. It would be winter in a matter of weeks. She wondered where they'd ended up. To be certain, the young couple must have found someplace to suffer hell's furies by now.

And now supper was cold. And Zeke still out with his company. Devil knew what he had them performing, but she'd be undamned if she was going to eat soup cold. She'd earned better. Through the height of Zeke's freewheeling bohemianism, when she'd had to appease the old rogue's every whim and simultaneously field the undying threats of the superstitious fascist down the road. Hardly a week going by without some fulmination against their conduct, the empty blackmailing menace about siccing the Feds on them. His kids vandalizing their property, ransacking the shed, kicking over bee-hives, scrawling mock curses in their very goats' blood on their own front door until she worked up the pluck and painted it that hideous red.

Such lifetimes of maintenance. And withal, they'd lost every-thing. And who'd been the one expected to keep it together? Who'd been the one with the plans? To dig deeper. Think broader. Go underground.

She'd been the one to put her foot down when it came to cats, and she'd be scorched by holy water if she were going to dine desolate that night, forsaken by way of her infernal design and innovation, of supporting her man, of sacrificing for… What? Or ever again.

Eunice put on her boots. Her feet had swollen from the change in weather, and she had to sit on the ground. She didn't relish getting older. It was not a good challenge. She couldn't even say how old she was. She'd stopped counting after everyone from the guild who hadn't already dropped dead got paranoid about cops and left.

It was dark. The only light beyond the main house flickered upslope. Smoke writhing in the chimney. Faint cracks of pressurized wood came into earshot as she made her ascent.

David Fishkind 191

Weatherstripping coiled at her feet like a perverse serpent. She opened the door with the weight of her body, backfirst. She hadn't been in the house on the hill in some months. She didn't like to interrupt, but she'd been waiting for over an hour and a half and had reheated the soup once more than she could dismiss.

The typewriter still settled on the butcher block, collecting cobwebs. A piece of paper was loaded, but no text appeared on it. She suspected he hadn't had a chance to begin.

Zeke moved fast these days, now well into his second century. When she'd met him he was all about having fun. He'd blathered on about the antics of theater. About going back to the city and taking Broadway by storm.

He seemed to have accepted that fun couldn't last.

Eunice inspected the fire. She turned the embers so they wouldn't extinguish themselves while she was subterranean. Then she pulled the floor hatch and dropped down to the crawl space.

On her knees, she jostled the flashlight from her apron and switched it on. She shone it about, searching for the scuttle. They'd gotten sloppy. She pushed the remains of canine vertebrae away with her wrist, padding about. From the time they'd put her blueprints to work, she'd had trouble locating the furtive passageway. Another testament to her skills of secretion.

At last her hand clenched cold metal. She twisted the frame until it released. Air escaped, and the soft thrum of piano trickled through.

She'd hoped Zeke would be already scaling his way out the other side. She spat loathsome obscenities under her breath, engulfed by ire eras in the festering, of how selfish he was, forgetting supper, carrying on like their whole existence were some million-act comedy, and not a tragedy of indefatigable errors. It would feel good to disturb his *joie de vivre*. *Libérant*.

She snorted at the word. As though it had wriggled pathetically begging for mercy from her womb to her rectum, regurgitating amid ghastly consciousness.

Eunice descended the ladder. Her boots struck stale earth. She was impressed with how solidly he'd managed to maintain it. She wondered how much help he'd gotten installing the ultramodern stainless steel beams she regarded along the shaft.

The piano grew louder then. A ragtimey, dissonant, minor progression.

—I hate you, a voice screamed.

—Now now, Zeke cooed.

—I'm going to kill you!

Unclear if the wail's source belonged to man or woman. In either case, its vocal cords shredded to their limits. Zeke giggled. She'd come at the right time. At worst, the players would appreciate it.

—From the top, Zeke sang.

Chains rattled and clanged. The shaft was fragrant. Eunice must have been more or less beneath her reconstituted fox soup. Reflective strip lights threaded through the steel supports and dimly illumined the corridor. Skeletons, mold, putrescence. But she was almost at the scaffold, and she could feel the mortals' warmth.

When she entered stage left, no one knew. The theater opened up with arched ceilings to reveal the rotten, split ends of roots. Worms and maggots impelled their segments through it and fell to the stony packed dirt, by bodies, which synchronously imprecated Zeke, spoke their lines with verve, and entered rhapsodic fits of weeping and hysterical laughter.

The kiln emanated heat from behind the piano. Its rusty tin smokeshaft depositing soot out the stump aboveground. She searched for the single man. The writer, supposedly. But they all looked the same. Mud and feces. Gaunt hipbones. Sunken cheeks.

It was a matter of time. And for a long time, everything and everyone had, to her, looked the same.

Zeke played the piano. The prisoners howled.

—Better, better. Almost there, sopranos. Altos, that's your cue, come in... Now!

He signaled to something, then shivered as it endeavored to trill.

—Ezekial, she uttered.

He stopped playing.

—What, he said, glaring at the keys.

—Supper's been ready two hours. You've gone long. It's time to break.

Zeke stood up directly. He didn't try to object.

—That's all for today, folks. Take five. I'll see you in the morning. We've got a hit on our hands, I've got to believe it. And you...

He pointed over his shoulder, still squinting into the original, genuine elephantine ivories.

—Mr. Fishkind. I want to applaud you on your hard work. We're getting there. It'll be a tough winter, but we'll make you a John Proctor yet.

With great effort, Zeke rose from the piano bench and limped over to Eunice.

—And you, he said. —Thanks for supper. But don't think I've forgotten for a minute. You owe me an Abigail Williams.

She put a hand on his arm, and he escorted her through the shaft, backlit by the glimmer of the incandescent kiln.

—Rent's due, Eunice said.

*

Oh, for all that, and many interludes later, she couldn't reach a conclusion. She still searched for an answer.

She wrested him for assessments, impressions, theoretical loops. Was it her sneeze? Or when she'd appeared unmasked, falsely innocent? The broken glove? What could the woman have meant by *virtually paragons*? Her fingers gnarled in perpetual air quotes.

She blamed who she was. Who he was. She couldn't bear to look at the puppy, it burdened her soul. She blamed anything to which she could train her waning editorial probes.

He lambasted her, silently. And himself, too, for holding on to such frivolity. Because not a night passed when, noting the delicate susurrus of dislodged litter crumbs, as he fitfully tossed into nightmare-racked slumber, he stupidly, cannily, and rightly blamed the cat.

Even after she'd found them a quaint colonial cottage, higher along on a taller hill in a more rugged tract of the very same valley as Zeke, Eunice, and their infamous, ever-growing cast. They were plagued.

CONTRIBUTORS

Aiden Arata is a writer, director and internet artist from Los Angeles. She's written for *BOMB*, *Mask*, *The Rumpus*, *The Fanzine*, and others. Her content has been featured in outlets including *Vice*, *The Cut*, and *Harper's Bazaar*. She lives on the internet at @aidenarata.

Nathan Dragon's work has been in *NOON Annual*, *Hotel*, *Sleepingfish*, *Fence*, and *New York Tyrant*. And Dragon co-runs a publishing project called Blue Arrangements.

David Fishkind is a writer and editor. In 2021, he co-founded the *Cheerio Review* with Lily Bartle. He lives in Massachusetts.

Rindon Johnson is an artist and poet. He is the author of *Nobody Sleeps Better Than White People* (Inpatient, 2016), the VR book, *Meet in the Corner* (Publishing-House.Me, 2017), *Shade the King* (Capricious, 2017) and forthcoming, *The Law of Large Numbers: Black Sonic Abyss* (Chisenhale, Inpatient, SculptureCenter 2021). He was raised on the ancestral lands of the Miwok people in Marin County, he lives in Berlin.

Aristilde Kirby is a being constellation of given human category [poet]. She has published this [*Daisy & Catherine* (Belladonna*, 2017)], that [*Sonnet Infinitesimal / Material Girl* (Black Warrior

Review & Best American Experimental Writing, 2020)], & the third *[Daisy & Catherine²*. (Auric Press, 2021)]. More contemporary affairs include this², [Mairead Connect Radio Club: Point A, a radio play for Montez Press Radio], that², [The Envoyelle: Notes on A Conditional Form, an essay on poetic form for Montez Press] & the third² [Crush Blossom / Crash Blossom, an essay about the global cut flower trade for Illiberal Arts, a group exhibition at the Haus der Kulturen der Welt in Berlin, curated by Kerstin Stakemeier & Anselm Franke.] She has a master's degree from the Milton Avery Graduate School of The Arts, Bard College.

Tao Lin is the author of *Leave Society* (Vintage, 2021)and other books. He edits Muumuu House and lives in Hawaii.

Chris Molnar is co-founder of the Writer's Block bookstore in Las Vegas. He is also co-founder and editorial director of Archway Editions, and editor of the *Unpublishable* anthology (Archway Editions, 2020) .

Vi Khi Nao's work includes poetry, fiction, film, play, and cross-genre collaboration. She is the author of the novel, *Fish in Exile* (Coffee House, 2016), the story collection *A Brief Alphabet of Torture* (winner of the 2016 FC2's Ronald Sukenick Innovative Fiction Prize) and of four poetry collections: *Human Tetris* (11:11, 2019), *Sheep Machine* (Black Sun Lit, 2018), *Umbilical Hospital* (1913 Press, 2017), and *The Old Philosopher* (winner of the 2014 Nightboat Prize). Her poetry collection, *A Bell Curve Is A Pregnant Straight Line*, and her short stories collection, *The Vegas Dilemma*, are forthcoming from 11:11 Press Summer and Fall 2021 respectively. She was the fall 2019 fellow at the Black Mountain Institute. www.vikhinao.com

Elle Nash is the author of the short story collection *Nudes* (SF/LD, 2021) and the novel *Animals Eat Each Other* (Dzanc Books, 2018), featured in *O - The Oprah Magazine* and hailed by *Publishers Weekly* as a 'complex, impressive exploration of obsession and desire.' Her work appears in *Guernica*, *BOMB*, *The Nervous Breakdown*, *Literary Hub*, *The Fanzine*, *Volume 1 Brooklyn*, *New York Tyrant* and elsewhere. She is a founding editor of *Witch Craft Magazine* and a fiction editor at both *Hobart Pulp* and *Expat Literary Journal*.

Gina Nutt is the author of the essay collection *Night Rooms* (Two Dollar Radio, 2021) and the poetry collection *Wilderness Champion* (Gold Wake Press, 2014). She earned her MFA from Syracuse University. Her writing has appeared in *Cosmonauts Avenue*, *Joyland*, *Ninth Letter*, and other publications.

Brad Phillips is an artist and writer based in Miami Beach. His critically acclaimed short story collection *Essays & Fictions* was published in 2019 by Tyrant Books. His first novel, *Stop Dying*, will be released in 2023.

Sam Pink is a blithering dunderhead.

Darina (Dasha) Sikmashvili was born in Lubny, Ukraine and raised in Brooklyn, New York. As of fall 2020, Darina is pursuing her MFA at Helen Zell Writers Program in Ann Arbor, Michigan.

Her writing has been published at *New World Writing*, *X-R-A-Y*, & *The Common*. She's at work on a novel. "This Is What I Have to Show for Life" won the John Wagner Prize at the University of Michigan in 2021. www.sikmashvili.com

B.R. Yeager reps Western Massachusetts. He is the author of *Negative Space* (Apocalypse Party, 2020), *Amygdalatropolis* (Schism Press, 2017) and *Pearl Death* (Inside the Castle, 2020).

ACKNOWLEDGEMENTS

Thank you to Chris Molnar for all his efforts related to the publication of this book, as well as for his help producing the NDA reading series with me at Stories bookstore in Los Angeles. Thank you to Connor Goodwin for the title.

MORE FROM ARCHWAY EDITIONS

Ishmael Reed – *The Haunting of Lin-Manuel Miranda*
Unpublishable (edited by Chris Molnar and Etan Nechin)
Gabriel Kruis – *Acid Virga*
Erin Taylor – *Bimboland*
Mike Sacks – *Randy*
Mike Sacks – *Stinker Lets Loose*
Paul Schrader – *First Reformed*
Archways 1 (edited by Chris Molnar and Nicodemus Nicoludis)
Brantly Martin – *Highway B: Horrorfest*
Stacy Szymaszek – *Famous Hermits*
cokemachineglow (edited by Clayton Purdom)
Ishmael Reed – *Life Among the Aryans*
Alice Notley – *Runes and Chords*

Archway Editions can be found at your local bookstore or ordered directly through Simon & Schuster.

Questions? Comments? Concerns? Send correspondence to:

Archway Editions
c/o powerHouse Books
220 36th St., Building #2
Brooklyn, NY
11232